Behind the Attic Wall

Behind the Attic Wall

Sylvia Cassedy

THOMAS Y. CROWELL   NEW YORK

for Michael and Timothy

Behind the Attic Wall
Copyright © 1983 by Sylvia Cassedy

Designed by Joyce Hopkins

7 8 9 10

Library of Congress Cataloging in Publication Data
Cassedy, Sylvia.
  Behind the attic wall.

  Summary: In the bleak, forbidding house of her
great-aunts, neglected twelve-year-old orphan Maggie
hears ghostly voices and finds magic that awakens in
her the capacity to love and be loved.
  [1. Orphans—Fiction.   2. Ghosts—Fiction.
3. Family life—Fiction]   I. Title.
PZ7.C268515Be   1983   [Fic]   82-45922
ISBN 0-690-04336-8
ISBN 0-690-04337-6 (lib. bdg.)

Part I

PROLOGUE

Today was the Anniversary: May fourteenth.

Last year they had all promised one another that they would meet again on this day and on every Anniversary, forever.

Now look. One year later and she was hundreds of miles away, sitting alone in a small room, leaning her forehead against the window, doing nothing, mostly. While they, the others, were . . . what were they doing, anyway?

Celebrating, probably. Celebrating without her. Sitting at the table, just as they had all sat last year, sipping ice cream from the edges of those tiny spoons and eating bits of cake from those little plates. Laughing. In a little while they would go out into the garden and unwrap their presents among the roses. Except that without her there couldn't be any presents. No new ones, anyway, and last year's had been ruined the day of the party. Come to think of it, without her there couldn't be any cake either.

Afterward they would get up from the table and play games. Maybe they would play the same game they had all played a year ago, the one that was the first and last they had ever played together, all of them, in that room next to the garden. Blindman's buff.

Maybe not. Maybe they would decide against it, remembering her, remembering that she was no longer there to play it with them.

She stared out the window.

Maybe the others had forgotten the Anniversary altogether.

Maybe they were spending the day as they always did, walking out among the roses, reading aloud from the newspaper, passing the bread and butter at teatime, saying crazy things.

Maybe they had forgotten her.

She rubbed her breath from the window with her fist.

There were no roses in this new garden. It was hardly a garden at all—just a backyard, really—and instead of a set of wicker furniture grouped in front of a wall of flowers there was a single aluminum lawn chair with nylon webbing that had begun to fray and that left scratches on the backs of your knees. The two little girls playing on the prickly grass caught sight of her face now and were smiling those smiles she had learned, after almost a year, to like. To love, really. Funny, crooked, friendly smiles. In a moment the two little sisters— her *sisters now, because she had finally begun to call their parents Mother and Father—would be up in her room.*

"Tell us about Adelphi Hills," they would say. "Tell us about

the old house and the scary rooms and the great big garden. *Tell us about your first day, and about how you went into all those rooms and took all that stuff that didn't belong to you."* They always asked that. *"Tell us about how you got caught in the garden with the necklace and all those other things."*

And she would tell them. She would tell them about how she arrived at Adelphi Hills with everything she owned stuffed into a duffel bag. She would tell them about the parlor with the little china ballerina locked behind glass doors, and she would tell them about the garden with the broken swing—broken by her—and the birches leaning like ghosts against the sky. She would tell them about taking things that weren't hers. She would even tell them about the empty room and the unused schoolroom with its rows of desks bolted to the floor. But she wouldn't tell them everything. She wouldn't tell them about the Anniversary, and she wouldn't tell them about the other room and the other garden. She wouldn't tell anyone about that. Ever.

CHAPTER ONE

⋘⦂⋙

The man waiting at the station when she first stepped off the train was the tallest person she had ever seen. His round black hat moved like a planet above the crowd, and the silver knob of his walking stick hovered just below it like a moon as he made his way toward her on the platform.

He looked her full in the face. "I'm looking for Margaret Ann Turner," he said. "I don't suppose you would have any information on where I might find her?"

No. Yes. How were you supposed to answer a question like that? "That's me," but he was already swinging her canvas duffel bag onto his shoulder, and she realized that he had known who she was all along. She wondered what description he had been given. Brown beret, brown coat, brown socks, ugly face? Bony legs, untied shoes, sandpaper knees, rotten temper? He was examining her carefully now. "You're quite certain that you are Margaret Ann Turner," he asked, "and not someone else with the same name?"

Another unanswerable question.

"It's Maggie," she said.

"Maggie!" he exclaimed. "Perfect!"

Perfect for me is what he means. Drab girl, drab name.

"I love the name Maggie," he went on, and she glanced up at him suspiciously—nobody loved the name Maggie—but his face was serious. "It makes your teeth feel good to say it. Maggie, Maggie, Maggie. It feels like eating peanuts. Try it," and he paused, waiting for her to recite her name aloud.

She turned away, but she did try anyway, to herself, and she felt a surprising tingle around her upper molars. Maybe like eating peanuts, maybe not; she couldn't really remember what peanuts tasted like.

"I am your uncle Morris," he said. "There is nothing remarkable about the name Morris at all, although I am told there is a chair by that name and also a dance. I can't imagine why anyone looking around for a name to give his chair would finally settle on Morris, can you?"

Maggie said nothing, and stood still, her eyes on the ground, while he continued to scrutinize her. "North Wellington Academy for Girls," he read from the emblem on her beret. "Is that really a girls' school you have on your head?" he asked. "If it is, its architecture seems strange. For one thing, there are no windows."

She would make it clear to him that she didn't enjoy being teased. "It's a hat," she said icily. She removed it from her head and, rolling it into a tube, slid it into her coat pocket.

"Ah," Uncle Morris replied. "A hat. Imagine having a girls' school in a hat."

Maggie made no reply and followed him as he made his way across the station platform to the lot where his car was parked. He laid her duffel bag carefully in the backseat and held the door open for her. As soon as the car began to move, she started to pick out letters of the alphabet from storefronts and billboards, getting quickly from A to I, but it was a while before she found a J, and soon the town was behind them, the signs grew sparser and sparser, and she gave up before reaching K.

"And now, Maggie," Uncle Morris said suddenly, "you must tell me something about yourself."

People were always saying that: "Tell me about yourself." There was nothing to tell. She had been in eight—no, nine— places to live and had been thrown out of all of them. Usually for "poor adjustment," which meant kicking people or stealing. Now she was going to stay with some aunts—*great*-aunts, actually—whose names she didn't even know and who lived in a place she had never heard of. Uncle Morris turned his face to her, waiting for her answer.

"I'm twelve," she finally said.

"Twelve!" he exclaimed. "How very nice," and he returned his eyes to the road. "Would that be inches or dollars?"

She glanced up at him. "What?"

"Twelve inches or twelve dollars?"

"Years," she answered.

"Twelve years! As old as that!" He paused for a moment. "How do you keep your hair from going gray?" and he turned to her again, expecting a reply, but this time she didn't answer.

"What else?" he asked.

She looked out the window. "What else *what*?"

"What else is there to tell about yourself? What do you wonder about? Do you ever wonder, for example, if everything that looks green to you is really everybody else's red?"

Maggie turned from the window and looked at him. She had wondered that once. What if the grass and the trees and the woolen skirt of last year's school uniform, all the things that were called green, really looked red or blue to everybody else? It was a scary idea, crazy really, and it surprised her to hear someone else—an adult, too—give voice to it.

"Have you ever wondered that?" he asked again.

"No," she answered, and she moved her knees aside when his hand came down on the knob of the gearshift rising from the floor.

They were in open country now, and Maggie narrowed her eyes until they were nearly shut, making the road ahead jump back and forth and shimmer like a fish.

"Do you keep a diary?" Uncle Morris asked suddenly.

She turned to look at him. How did he know about that? She had kept a diary once. When she was at Mrs. Malloy's. Four schools ago. Five. A black leather diary. Except it wasn't real leather and it wasn't a real diary. And it wasn't hers. It was an appointment book, and she had taken it from the headmistress's desk. Many of the pages had already been filled in, but there were some that remained empty, and she had used those to write on. Each page was divided into hours, from 6 A.M. to 11 P.M., and you were supposed to write down things you had to do that day, but she used it for writing things after they had happened, not before. Seven A.M.: Got up. Brushed teeth. Got dressed. Eight A.M.: Ate breakfast. Nine A.M.: Threw up. One day, though, she had drawn a line through all the hours and written only one message: Built a wall of flowers. She *had* built a wall of flowers, or had tried to, that day. She had pulled all the flowers from the beds surrounding the school building, every single flower from every single bed, and had arranged them like a row of bricks—yellows on reds, reds on yellows—and when she was all finished she would stand behind it, behind the wall of flowers, and let no one in. But she had run out of flowers when they were just a few inches off the ground, and Mrs. Malloy herself had caught her. That was her last day at that school, and her diary ended on that page.

"Do you keep a diary?" Uncle Morris asked again.

"No."

"Why is that?"

She shrugged. "There's nothing to write."

"But I only wondered if you *kept* one, not if you wrote in it. I throw all of mine away."

Maggie decided not to answer his questions anymore. They made no sense and everything she said was wrong. Instead, she concentrated on the scenery, taking a strand of her hair as she did so and sucking it to a sharp point.

The open countryside was giving way now to a small town; the roads leading off to the right and left had street signs, not just route numbers, and now and then there was a row of stores. Maggie found her K on a No Parking sign. Soon they were passing houses, large ones with wide lawns, and small ones, too, with their numbers written out in script over the doorways: one hundred eighty-three, one hundred eighty-five. In the distance was the fuzzy roofline of a large gray building. A school, maybe. Or a factory.

"We'll be there pretty soon," Uncle Morris said, and Maggie suddenly wondered about the house she was being taken to and the two people who lived there.

Once, long ago, she had lived with a mother and a father—a *real* mother and father, not the foster kind—in a plain brown house with a wooden porch in front and a miracle of a garden out back. Since that time every house in her imagination took on the arrangement of that early one, with its narrow hallway downstairs (living room on the right, dining room on the left, kitchen in the rear) and its three bedrooms all in a row upstairs. It was the house in which she placed the Three Bears and Little Red Ridinghood's grandmother and Jo, Meg, Amy, and Beth. It was the house in which she placed all her old schoolmates when they left her behind on the boarding school lawn and drove out the gates with their mothers and fathers for weekend visits. It was the house in which she placed herself when she was told that she would be looked after by two great-aunts who had agreed, when no one else had, to take her in and let her live with them.

She'd be taken up the front porch steps of this new house with the living room on the right and the dining room on the left, and her two great-aunts would be waiting for her. "Great-aunt" had a kind of fairy-tale ring to it, and she thought of two great women in great billowing dresses with great white aprons and smiling great white smiles. When she stood before them on the wooden porch they would kiss her and say, "What a lovely face," and then they would tell her how happy they were to have her with them because they always wanted a girl of their own just like her, and they would take her into the kitchen and give her cocoa and cookies.

The car was now winding up a long hill. Dense trees grew on either side, and Maggie could see no houses at all, nothing, in fact, except the fuzzy outline of the building whose rooftop had appeared earlier against the sky—the factory, or whatever it was. In the next moment it came into full view, a massive stone structure with rows of narrow windows and a heavy double door at the head of wide stone steps. A prison, probably, Maggie thought, squinting at it and sucking on another strand of hair.

"Well, there it is," Uncle Morris announced.

Maggie sat up. There *what* is?

"There's where you're going to live."

There? She was going to live in that building? But that was an institution! A prison! What of the house with the front porch? And what of the two great-aunts? A rich liquid sprang from the sides of her mouth. "I have to throw up," she said, and Uncle Morris drew the car to the side of the road. He leaned across her to open the door and then gazed out the windshield while she bent over the roadside.

"Here," he said, when she had closed the door and he had started up the hill again, and he handed her a white handkerchief from his breast pocket. She wiped her mouth and nose, and then didn't know what to do with the crumpled cloth in her hand. Give it back to him, sour as it was, and let him return it to his pocket? Hold on to it herself and let its smell rub into her own moist palms? What? Finally, looking straight ahead, she raised it slowly to the edge of the window and released it, turning at last to see it flutter, like an injured sea gull, in the dust at the side of the road.

Neither of them spoke until they stopped on a circular driveway before the large building, so large its shadow cast a chill on their car and blackened the surrounding trees.

"Well," Uncle Morris said. "Here we are."

CHAPTER TWO

❧§❧

The first thing Maggie's eye rested on as she stared out the car window was the brass plaque next to the huge double doors. ADELPHI HILLS ACADEMY, it said, and she knew that once again she had been tricked. There were no great-aunts and there was no house. She was being delivered to another boarding school. Of all the school buildings she had ever seen, though, this was by far the most menacing. Nothing stirred anywhere—no curtain, no leaf, no spiral of smoke— and no color broke the smoothness of its walls. It was like a photograph in black and white, fallen from the pages of some forgotten album.

Uncle Morris unfolded himself from the car, reached into

the back seat for the duffel bag, and ceremoniously opened Maggie's door, freezing like a footman, but she didn't move. She wouldn't get out. She would stay here in the car until somebody drove her back to the train station and sent her back to . . . back where? Uncle Morris, balancing the duffel bag on his shoulder, turned up the walk and slowly approached the wide stone steps. Where could she go? Her uncle paused now and turned around to look at her. The duffel bag tipped him slightly to one side, and he rested on his walking stick. Back where?

"You'll have to walk faster than that if you hope to make the front steps before nightfall," he called out, but she remained in her seat, her eyes fixed on the great stone wall. Back where? Back to North Wellington Academy for Girls, where, just the day before, the headmistress had told her she was a disgrace to the school? Back to the school before that, where she had lasted only a week? Back to the school before that? Back where? Back nowhere, that's where, and slowly Maggie got out of the car. Her legs were unsteady and she grew dizzy for a moment. She leaned against the car door and watched her duffel bag continue its progress up the front walk.

Once again she looked over the broad wall of stone in front of her, and for a quick moment she caught a glimpse of what seemed to be a red head following her arrival from a high window, but then the wall was still, and only a sunbeam, caught on a snag of glass, burst into a flash of orange before it escaped and the windows were dark and empty once more.

Uncle Morris had reached the steps now, and very slowly, keeping her eyes on her feet, she started along the walk. She didn't raise her eyes until a long time later, when she reached the steps. There, on either side, stood a gray stone urn, round and fat as a witch's cauldron. If she was quick, she could climb into one of them while her uncle's back was turned, and he wouldn't know where she was. No one would. She could stay there until dark and then steal away. Away where?

She counted the steps as she climbed them—there were thirteen—and finally she stood behind her uncle at the double doors. In a moment she would hear the familiar sounds of a boarding school—scuffling on the stairway, footsteps overhead, voices in the next room, and, from some fenced play yard, a distant cry. Then she would see the girls themselves, the rows of uniformed girls, retreating down a hallway two by two; staring at a blackboard six to a row; eating mashed potatoes at a long green table. Always in rows. Some of them, knowing that a new girl was to arrive, would already have their eyes on the door.

At first Maggie could see nothing at all. They stood in total darkness, and there was silence all around. Just then, though, Uncle Morris reached for an overhead string and a dim orange glow lit up a long entrance hall. A small pale figure in a coat stood facing her. No, it was a figure in a mirror. It was her own figure. Straight ahead was a strange apparatus with protruding arms like a dragon's—a clothes rack it was—and it had a full-length mirror in its back panel. Her own reflection hung fragilely within its frame, and she stared at the white face, the brown coat, the pale legs "thin as straws," as one of her headmistresses used to say. Uncle Morris hung his bowler on one of the dragon arms and his walking stick on another. The duffel bag lay collapsed on the floor like a sleeping dog.

Something stirred at the far end of the hall, and Maggie stepped back. Two figures, one in brown, the other in green, suddenly emerged. They grasped one another, as though each would fall if the other let go, and stopped at a distance from Maggie, holding her in a long, fixed gaze. She had been looked at like that before, always on her first day at a new place and always by the headmistress. These, then, were the headmistresses—*two* of them this time!—and she waited while the two pairs of eyes traveled down her body, starting with her hair, wet and stiff from sucking, moving down to her shapeless coat with the beret bulging from its pocket, dwelling for a moment on her socks, both brown but not of the same pair, and settling finally on her shoelaces with their missing tips and tufts of loose thread.

"Here she is," Uncle Morris announced, and she found herself being steered across the floor. "Margaret Ann Turner, but she pronounces it Maggie. She's twelve inches high—no, that's not right. She's twelve something and she arrived with a girls' school on her head, but she's since transferred it to her pocket." He turned to her now. "Your great-aunt Lillian. Your great-aunt Harriet."

These were her great-aunts? The great-aunts in the big dresses and aprons who were going to greet her on the front porch and kiss her and tell her how happy they were she had come to live with them? The great-aunts were headmistresses? She was going to have to call the headmistresses Aunt this and Aunt that, while everyone else in the school called them Miss something or other? Her stomach fell.

One of the two figures, the one in green, started to approach her and in a moment she was lowering her face toward Maggie's. This was to be the kiss, and Maggie tightened her teeth, waiting for a wet mouth to moisten her cheek, but the face stopped an inch or two away and held still. Now she was taking Maggie by the arm—to lead her where? Maggie wondered. Nowhere. She was only holding on to Maggie's thin wrist, encircling it with her thumb and middle finger and looking at it closely, measuring its circumference.

"Skin and bones," she finally pronounced. "Skin and bones," and she dropped the arm, letting it swing like a loose rope at Maggie's side.

Maggie turned away from the staring face and listened for the sounds of the other girls in their rooms behind the walls and above the stairs. Everything was still, and in the dim light she could see no one approaching but her other great-aunt, the one in brown, who now stood next to the figure in green and joined her in examining Maggie's face.

"Where is her hat?" she demanded. "Her ears shouldn't be exposed to the air on a day like this. She'll get earache."

The aunt in green spoke: "There's no color to her face."

The aunt in brown: "Look how she stands. Her spine must be crooked."

"It's the diet. They never feed them properly in those places."

"And the air. They breathe stale air all day."

They looked like hand puppets when they spoke, the kind Maggie had once seen on a television screen, with mouths that opened wide to let words out and then snapped shut, tight as a duck's bill.

"Her hair is in strings."

"It hasn't been washed in months."

"Look at the color of her knees."

"Black."

"She could do with a scrubbing from top to bottom." And with this pronouncement both mouths shut, and only the heads moved, up and down, twice, three times, as though they were scrubbing her clean already, with their noses.

"Tell her lunch will be ready in half an hour," the green one finally said to Uncle Morris.

Uncle Morris bent to her ear. "I have something to tell you," he said. "Lunch will be ready in half an hour. Ready for what, though, I cannot say." He turned to the two retreating figures. "Shall I await a reply?" he asked, but they didn't answer, and in a moment they had stepped out of the glow of the orange light and into the darkness at the end of the hall.

"First," Uncle Morris said now to Maggie, "we will hang up your coat," and he led her to the clothes rack with the protruding dragon arms and full-length mirror. Maggie stood before it and looked at her reflection as she had just been looked at by her two aunts, letting her eye run down the hair in wet strings, the thin face, the black knees, the unmatched socks. Cautiously she took her left wrist in the fingers of her right hand and measured its width. Skin and bones, she thought.

"Would you like to wear your coat while I hang it up?" Uncle Morris broke in. "Or would you prefer to remove it first?"

Maggie shifted her glance quickly to the image of his face in the mirror. He was bending down and his head was situated some six inches below the reflection of his bowler on its hook, making him look like a cartoon figure whose hat had just popped off in a moment of surprise. Without replying, she removed her coat and handed it to him, watching as he placed it between two heavy woolen garments, one brown, one black, where it hung like a loose sack of skin on the bone of an outstretched arm. "And now," he said, extending his own arm, "we will sit in the parlor while your two excellent relatives prepare their usual culinary delights."

The parlor. All these places had parlors. The main thing about parlors was that you were never allowed into them, except maybe on the day you arrived, and the next main thing about them was that they were always gray. Gray plush sofas that no one got to sit on, gray plush chairs, gray footstools with gray cushions undented by any foot, gray walls papered with gray feathered prints.

The parlor that she gazed into now from its doorway was also gray. The furniture was gray, the walls were gray, and the curtains holding back the daylight at the windows were gray.

"This is the green room," Uncle Morris announced, but his strange jokes confused her and she didn't respond. There was no green in the room at all, not even in the rug, which was unexpectedly patterned with faded red and blue flowers and vines winding in elaborate knots.

"It's because of them," Uncle Morris continued, and he pointed to two large portraits in identical frames, one of a man, the other of a woman, each wearing the clothing of long ago. There was no green in either picture. There was no color at all, in fact, except for a reddish tinge in the man's hair and a red-patterned cloth at the woman's wrist. Everything else was black and white—severe white faces, and clothing so dark Maggie couldn't see its outline against the black background. "They were the first headmaster and headmistress of the Academy," Uncle Morris explained, "and their name was Green."

Maggie stared into their faces for a moment, stiff faces with straight, thin lips and narrow eyes. Headmistress faces, she thought, and she turned back to the rest of the room. A fan of magazines lay on a nearby table, and she read their titles: *Health, Today's Health, Nutrition Digest, Body and Mind, Food and You.* Next to them was a careful pile of *National Geographics*, yellow and black. All parlors had *National Geographics* that no one read. Opposite was a curio cabinet with rows of ivory elephants and, wonderfully, a china ballerina with peach-pink arms and an amazing skirt of china netting. Would she be kept in this new place long enough, Maggie wondered, to learn how to unlock the cabinet door and run her finger along the dancer's brittle, ruffled hem?

"She's been practicing that step for about a hundred years," Uncle Morris said, following her glance, "and she still hasn't mastered it. Think what it must be like to stand on one toe for a hundred years. For fifty years, even. Have you ever thought what that must be like?" He turned his head, waiting for Maggie's answer.

"No," she said, not looking at him.

"No? Not once? You never contemplated standing on one toe your whole life through, never once changing toes, not even at night when no one was around to see?"

"It's just a piece of china." She shrugged.

"And"—Uncle Morris looked at her closely, so closely that she stepped back—"have you ever wondered what it would be like to be 'just a piece of china'?"

Actually, she had wondered things like that. What was it like to be something that didn't feel or see or hear? What was it like to be the chair she sat on or the lamp she read by or the table she ate from or the bed she lay in? What was it like to be a table and not *know* you were a table? What was it like not to be anything at all? What was it like to be dead?

"I'm told it's rather pleasant," Uncle Morris said, and she looked up at him sharply. "Being a piece of china, provided you don't have to spend all your time on one toe."

Maggie stared at the rug, tracing the wanderings of a vine from one border to the other—in, out, around; in, out, around—until her eye grew weary and the pattern jumped. Uncle Morris had fallen silent, and there was no sound at all from beyond the walls. Where *was* everybody? She strained her ears: no shuffle of footsteps, no rustle of clothing, no shout, no whisper, no sob even. Nothing. She slid a hank of hair into her mouth, twisting it with her tongue until it was stiff and sticky, and then stood without moving until a voice broke in with the suddenness of an alarm: "Lunch!" It was one of the headmistresses calling from down the hall, and Uncle Morris sprang up to offer Maggie his arm. "Lunch," he said, his elbow extended, but she kept her hands at her sides, while he led the way through long, silent hallways, his arm still raised as though he were reading a watch or carrying a length of window curtain.

CHAPTER THREE

❧⚜❧

It was always the same, the first meal on arrival day at a new boarding school. She would stand a long while in the doorway of a dining room crowded with girls all dressed alike, all talking, all shouting, all clattering their metal trays against the long metal tables. Soon, though, a few girls, those near the front of the room, would catch sight of her and fall silent. Then, little by little, the silence would move out in a ripple toward the opposite wall, and in time everyone would be still, staring intently at her, the new girl, the stranger.

There would be no place set for her, and she would stand in the doorway even longer while someone was sent for an extra chair and someone else went for a tray with a plate and fork. Then there would be no space for her chair, and she would wait while a row of girls would squeeze closer together, and finally she would walk to her new place at the corner where the table edge would jut into her chest and its leg bump her knee.

She continued to follow Uncle Morris down the hall with its dark, silent walls until he stopped at last at a closed door, and she listened for the lunchroom sounds she knew so well— voices, mostly, but clattering, too, and the crash of a chair.

The next minute the door was open and Maggie stood in a room with no one else in it at all.

A long table, longer than any Maggie had ever seen, and made not of gray metal but of polished wood, stood in the center of the room. It could have seated all eighteen girls in her class at the school she had just left, but there were only four chairs, one at each side, and four plates. A large chandelier hung from the ceiling, but it was not lit; the only light entered from two slender windows at the far end of the room, casting white oblongs, thin and cold, on the bare floor and across the table.

Suddenly a swinging door swept open, and one of the great-aunts, the one in green, came in with a tray of platters and bowls. In a moment she was gone and the other aunt, the brown one, came through the same door with a tray of her own. Back and forth they moved, first the green one and then the brown, like the little figures that tell the weather by popping in and out of a tiny wooden house.

Maggie was seated on one long side of the table, facing Uncle Morris. The aunt in green sat at the window end, and the aunt in brown sat at the other. Where, though, was everyone else? In some other lunchroom, probably. She was being given special treatment because this was her first day, and she was allowed to sit with the headmistresses in the formal dining room while the rest of the school crowded around metal tables in some basement lunchroom. She strained again for the sounds of voices, but there was silence all around.

Maybe everyone else had already eaten. She suddenly realized she had no idea what time it was. Maybe they had all eaten hours ago, at this very table, and were now hidden in upstairs rooms or scattered across unseen lawns. She stared into her plate: mashed potatoes, peas, a fried egg, a folded slice of bread and butter. To one side stood a mug of milk. A boarding school lunch. She lifted her fork. In two minutes she could take care of the whole thing, beginning with the egg yolk, which she stabbed at fiercely with her fork until it burst. Silently she watched as it bled across its surrounding white film and onto the plate. Sticky yellow blood, she thought, and she rubbed it dry with the edge of her bread. Next the potatoes. In one movement she swept them into a narrow wreath around the edge of her plate and buried everything else in their depths—the peas; the egg; the folded bread,

stained yellow now and beginning to shred. In a
the center of her plate was clean, and the two aun
think she had eaten most of her meal.

"Harriet," the aunt in green cried across the le
the table, "she isn't eating at all! She is taking no nouri
into her system!"

Uncle Morris scrambled to his feet. "A toast!" he
and he raised his water glass so high it almost collided
the crystal teardrops hanging from the chandelier. "A
to Margaret Ann Turner and to her system: may they sp
many happy years together!" He waved his glass several ti
as though he were writing something in the air with it, a
then put it to his lips.

The two aunts looked at him for only a second. "On
shouldn't wash down one's food with liquid," the green on
snapped. "Food cannot be properly digested unless it is properly chewed."

"What a lovely sentiment," Uncle Morris exclaimed, sitting
down again. "Is that something you just made up, Lillian,
or did you steal it from a book of proverbs?"

"Morris, be still," the aunt in brown said, and they all
fell silent.

Maggie stared at the pattern of birds and flowers that she
had revealed on her plate. In the other schools there were
no patterns on the dishes, and the silverware was plastic.
She held up the silver fork, sticky now with egg yolk, and

examined the heavy scrollwork on its handle. Then, with its prongs, she ran a wavy row of ridges around the surface of the mashed potatoes, in and out, in and out, like tire tracks in snow.

"Lillian," the brown aunt said, speaking across the length of the table, "look how she eats."

"She has no manners," the green aunt snapped. "She will have to be taught." She raised her head and began to speak as though she were on a platform. "It behooves us all," she proclaimed, "to respect the sensibilities of others by observing proper table manners at all times."

Behooves. That was headmistress talk. It behooves each and every one of us to keep our classrooms clean. It behooves us all to treat one another with common courtesy. It behooves us to shut up.

"Behooves?" Uncle Morris put his fork down. "BEE hooves?" His voice was unbelieving. "Maggie, did you hear that? Bees with hooves? All those bees out there are galloping around on *hooves*, while we just sit here at the dining table calmly eating our lunch? Think what will happen to the flowers! Finish eating, Maggie; we must go and rescue the roses before they all get bruised."

"Morris, stop being tiresome," the aunt in brown ordered, and for a long time nothing further was said. The two aunts bobbed over their plates like birds at a fountain, and Maggie spent the time trying to work a chocolate bar out of a pocket

in her skirt. It had been given to her as a going-away present the night before by one of the girls in her old boarding school. It wasn't exactly a present; she had taken it, but the girl said she could have it anyway. Keep it, the girl had said, for good luck. It had been her only good-bye—the cab that had come to take her to the station had been called for the night before and she had left before anyone else was up. The candy bar felt soft now, and its chocolate ran against her fingertips as she held it behind her back and undid the wrapper.

"Lillian," the aunt in brown said suddenly. "Explain the rules."

The rules. There were always rules. Usually they were hung on a sheet of paper inside the bedroom door. No eating anywhere except in the dining room. No going into the parlor. No talking after ten o'clock. No leaving your towel on the bathroom floor. No this, no that.

"There will be rules," the aunt in green was saying now. Aunt Lillian. Green, Lillian; brown, Harriet. Green, Lillian; brown, Harriet. Tomorrow, though, they'd be wearing different clothes and Maggie wouldn't be able to tell them apart. She looked more carefully at the green aunt and noticed that she had freckles. Thousands of freckles, in fact, all running together along her arms. Once, long ago, she had been told—by whom? her real mother? maybe—that freckle fairies came through the windows with tiny paintbrushes dipped in gold and speckled the noses of little children as they lay asleep. She thought now, instead, of a whole army of grotesque elves squeezing their paintpots and heavy brushes through the narrow windows of this massive stone building to stain her aunt's fleshy arms brown and tan, the colors of her own school clothes.

"There will be rules," Aunt Lillian with the freckles was saying now, "and they will be strictly adhered to." Maggie looked back into her plate. "You are permitted only in certain designated areas of the building." Next would come the part about no eating in the bedrooms.

"There are rules about food and drink," the aunt in brown put in. Brown, Harriet. Maggie turned to look at her. She was thinner and more wrinkled than her sister. The skin at her throat hung in folds like unpressed silk, and heavy lines like pencil strokes framed her mouth. She would be the meaner one, Maggie decided, but it didn't matter. Mean or nice, it was all the same: she would hate them both. And they would hate her. In fact, they already did.

"You will drink from eight to ten glasses of water each day," Aunt Harriet was saying, "and visit the bathroom every morning before breakfast." Maggie stared at her.

"You will eat a serving of protein at every meal," Aunt Lillian said from her end of the table, "and plenty of green and yellow vegetables every day." She pronounced "vegetables" with four syllables—vedge-a-ta-bulls—and "protein" with three—pro-tee-in. "Milk or a milk product three times a day and a carbohydrate twice." Maggie stared now at Aunt Lillian. She had seen all that somewhere on the side of a cereal box, and she wondered for a moment if her aunt were reading aloud. "Carbohydrates line the tubes."

What kind of rules *were* these, anyway? No place had rules about carbohydrates and yellow vegetables.

"Ten hours of sleep each night. You may listen to the radio for an hour after dinner. There is no television. Television weakens the mind."

All boarding schools had television. You could watch it for only a couple of hours after dinner, maybe, and you were usually being punished for something so that you couldn't watch it at all, but still it would be *there.* What kind of place *was* this?

"You will dress according to the weather and not the calendar. Warm leg coverings on cold days, and a woolen hat that covers the ears. Rubbers when it rains."

"You will not take anything unclean or unhealthful into your system."

Maggie brought the candy bar up to her lips now and ate it all at once. She scraped the last streaks of chocolate from the wrapper with her teeth and then, crushing it into a jagged ball, let it drop behind her chair to the floor. Finally she sucked the chocolate slowly from each finger, making loud kissing noises as she did so.

Both aunts rose.

"Look what she's doing!"

"She's a disgusting child."

The sweetness stung her throat, and she took a quick gulp of her milk, but the next moment she slammed the mug down on the table, her lips and gums burning. "It's hot!" she cried in surprise. They were the first words she had spoken since she had entered the dining room, and her voice cracked halfway through.

"The milk is warm," Aunt Lillian explained, not raising her voice. "The chill has been taken off. Cold milk shocks the system. Remember that."

Maggie gazed first at the two aunts and then at the thin ring of food edging her plate. In the next moment she seized her mug of milk and emptied it onto the design of birds and flowers. A creamy pond rippled against the banks of potatoes, and a pea set sail uncertainly to the opposite shore. "It's *hot*!" she shouted.

Both aunts rushed toward her. "She's ruined her meal!" Aunt Harriet cried.

"All that nutritious food!"

"Don't offer her any more. Let her go hungry until she learns."

"But she is malnourished."

"It can't be helped. Take her to her room."

Then Uncle Morris spoke for the first time since he had

been silenced earlier by Aunt Harriet. He gazed steadily at Maggie, struggling now as Aunt Lillian lifted her by the elbow and led her out of the room. "I think," he said slowly, and she felt his words at her back, "I think you are the right one after all," but she didn't pay attention to his words until a long time later.

CHAPTER FOUR

᎒᎒᎒

Maggie followed the green dress out of the dining room, through the long, dark passageways, and into the front hall. Their footsteps rang on the bare floors, and Maggie listened to them with the ears of the silent girls in their school uniforms, behind their doors—upstairs, downstairs, wherever they were—all thinking: Here she comes: the new girl. Maybe they had heard her shout in the dining room and were standing somewhere at open doors, pretending not to look when she finally passed by, but looking anyway, under lowered lids.

Her duffel bag lay against the clothes rack where Uncle Morris had left it, and she grabbed it by its neck, bumping it behind her on the chill wooden stairs to the second story.

The walls in the upstairs hall, like the walls she had seen everywhere else, were paneled in dark wood, with no daylight to brighten their grain. Aunt Lillian lit their way through the darkness by pausing here and there to pull on an overhead string, creating a dim orange circle on the floor that faded before it reached the walls.

There were heavy wooden doors on either side, but none of them were open and no girl stood within any of their frames. Maggie strained for the sound of a voice, the shuffle of a foot, but she heard nothing, and she continued along the hall, counting the doors on her fingers as she passed them. There were ten: ten wooden doors, all silent, all closed. Later, when no one was looking, she would open them all.

They stopped at a door at one end of the hall, and Aunt Lillian opened it, leading Maggie into her room. A deep chill, cold as the breath of a passing ghost, struck her as she entered, and she clasped her arms to silence a shiver. At first she could hardly see: The only window was curtained in heavy cloth and the walls were painted brown. Her aunt parted the curtain and Maggie looked around. The room would belong to her alone, she noticed; there was only one bed—a metal one, with a white cotton spread and a navy blanket folded into a rectangle across the foot. Most of the rooms in the other boarding schools had to be shared. Once, even, with eleven other girls, six beds to a wall.

A small sink stood in one corner, a writing desk in another, and a chest of drawers filled one narrow wall. The floor was bare. Who had been here last, she wondered, and why had she left? She shrugged. Someday—two weeks, a month, six months from now, after she had been thrown out—some other girl would stand shivering in this room and ask herself the same question.

"You will be expected to keep your room clean," Aunt Lillian was saying. "There are no servants here." No servants. That was strange. Boarding schools always had servants, except they weren't called that. They were called Mildred or Cora, and sometimes they would steal food for you from the kitchen when you were sent to your room without supper. "You will make your bed every day and sweep the dust off the floor. It is unwholesome to sleep in a room with dust in the air. Remove hairs from the sink so they do not clog the drains, and do not allow anything to accumulate on the surfaces."

Maggie didn't *have* anything to accumulate on the surfaces—no knickknacks, no stuffed animals, no photographs. Her duffel bag contained a tangle of gray-pink underwear and parts of old school uniforms. At the bottom lay a toothbrush and a comb. A ball-point pen. A deck of sticky cards held together with a rubber band. Nothing more.

"Your clothing is provided for you," her aunt said, and she opened the closet door to reveal a row of dark dresses hanging one beside another like a line of headless schoolgirls.

She lifted one from the pole and held it against Maggie's body. Maggie looked down at it: It reached far below her knees, and she could tell by the pale crease where a hem had been let out that it had once belonged to someone else. The fabric pricked her skin, and she wriggled away. "You will grow into it," her aunt said briskly, returning it to the closet, and she began next to remove garments from the dresser drawers. "Stand still," she ordered as she held one article of clothing after another against Maggie's shoulders or her waist or her legs.

"You will grow into these, too," Aunt Lillian said, but Maggie knew she wouldn't remain here long enough to grow into anything. "They were made for better-nourished children," and her aunt rolled each piece up and returned it to the drawer.

This, then, was what the other girls in the school wore: brown cotton stockings fastened by pink rubber buttons dangling from a garter belt, shapeless brown dresses, peach-pink underpants that came down to the knees, white slips, and yellowing undershirts with sleeves. She wouldn't wear any of it. She'd shove it all out of sight and wear her own clothes instead—the underpants with the torn seams and the socks that didn't match.

Aunt Lillian reached now into another drawer, and Maggie turned away, not wanting to see. "And now I have something else for you." A sudden change in her tone made Maggie look up anyway, and she found her aunt hiding something behind her back. "It's a surprise," she said, and there was excitement in her voice. "Can you guess what it is?" Maggie stared at her. "No," she said, and she turned away, but the next moment something was being thrust in front of her face, and she stepped back. It was a doll. A rubber baby doll, and she could see by its unblemished cheek and stiff dress that it was brand-new: a brand-new baby doll with a pink rubber face, a pale arc over each glass eye, a blond wig, and a crimson mouth smiling incongruously into the chill of the dark room. A *doll!*

"Do you like it?" Aunt Lillian whispered, bending over with what looked like the start of a smile. "I dressed it myself," and she lifted the doll's pink skirt to reveal a tiny pair of underpants edged in lace. "Here," she said. "It's for you," and the smile widened a little.

Maggie took the doll and stared at the pink rubber face with its pale painted eyebrows and smiling mouth. Did everybody who came to this place get a doll? All those girls in their brown dresses and stockings who would soon come out into the dark hall from wherever they were, did they all have dolls just like this, dressed in clothes far nicer than their own? With her thumb she pushed in the doll's rubber nose until its glass eyes bulged out in astonishment and its smile disappeared. "I don't play with dolls," she said. "They're dumb."

The small smile disappeared from Aunt Lillian's face, as though it, too, had been pushed out by a firm thumb, and a network of fine lines sprang from the corners of her mouth. She held Maggie in a shocked glare. Maggie stared back. She had learned that trick somewhere, probably from one of her old schoolmates: stare hard at people and they drop their eyes. Then they go away. It always worked. It worked now. In a moment Aunt Lillian was gone, closing the door behind her. "Skin and bones," Maggie heard her mutter. "And impudent besides. It was a great mistake, allowing her here. *Harriet!*"

"I don't play with *anything*," Maggie shouted after her. "Not anything!" and she squeezed the doll's body between both her hands. From somewhere within its hollows there came an answering cry like that of a cat, and Maggie dropped it to the floor.

CHAPTER FIVE

❧

Aunt Lillian's footsteps grew more distant, became whispers, were gone. The building fell silent. Maggie walked to the mirror over the sink. With her little fingers she stretched her lips out as far as they would go, shaping them into a sideways figure eight, a skinny dumbbell, a sliver, a slit. Farther and farther she pulled, until the skin on her lower lip cracked and a fine line of blood broke through. Now she brought her face closer and closer to the glass until her reflected eyes jumped together into one brown jelly bean afloat in the middle of her forehead. Ugly, she said, ugly, ugly, ugly, and she sat down on the bed.

What would happen next? How much longer would she sit here before someone came to get her? Who would come?

Some robust girl, probably, better nourished than she, in a brown dress that came just to her knee. She would knock at her door in an hour, two hours, saying, "You have to come now," and lead her to a class. But all at once Maggie remembered something: Today was Saturday. There were no classes. There were no special meals, even. Saturday was a quiet day. The older girls went into town on Saturday, to the five-and-ten, bringing back bottles of nail polish with names like Pink Grapefruit or Black Orchid and cards of bobby pins, their wavy bumps all lined up in perfect, shiny rows. But the other girls, the girls her age, wandered in ragged groups around the grounds, radios clamped to their ears, or stayed in their rooms and combed and combed their hair at the mirror.

Maggie went to the window seat and knelt on its bare wood. The garden outside was an immense stretch of grass, and she looked across its reaches for a sign of the returning girls—a row of heads, maybe, emerging from behind the flower bed or an indistinct blur moving among the trees and separating suddenly into a tangle of arms and legs. But nothing broke the stillness of the scene that hung behind the curtains like the backdrop of a play, and Maggie finally turned back to her room.

It wasn't quite true, what she had shouted to Aunt Lillian— that she didn't play anything. She did play things. She played solitaire with the deck of cards that lay at the bottom of her duffel bag. She played games in her head. She played caretaker. Caretaker was a game she had made up long ago, and she played it almost every day. She played it now, while she waited for the girls to return or for someone to come to her door.

She was a caretaker in her game, a caretaker of five imaginary girls, the Backwoods Girls she called them, all poorer, younger, dirtier, and uglier than she was herself. And dumber. They were all newly arrived from some unknown backwoods, and they knew nothing, nothing at all, of the ordinary things surrounding Maggie's life—of toothbrushes, even, or dresser drawers, and it was Maggie's job to explain things to them.

"Come here," Maggie called silently, and in an instant all five imaginary girls stood around her with their wondering stares. "What's this?" asked one, examining the wooden knobs on the dresser.

"That's a drawer," Maggie answered, not aloud, but in her head. "Pull on it and out it comes. See? Like this. Don't shove each other; there's room for all of you, and you can take turns."

"Ooh, what's inside?" they asked all at once.

"Beautiful things," Maggie answered, and she held up one of the long brown stockings.

"Ooh, what's that?"

"That's a stocking. Stockings are what rich people wear." She held it against her thigh. "To make their legs look beautiful. Like mine. Look. And they're also to keep your feet from sticking to your shoes."

The Backwoods Girls answered all at once. "Ooh, how wonderful!" Their responses were usually limited to those words, followed by a new question. "What's shoes?"

"Shoes are these things I have on my feet, with the laces. Look, I'll show you how they work."

"Ooh, how wonderful. And what's this?"

"That's underpants."

"What's underpants."

"Don't you even know what underpants are?" Maggie sighed in disgust, as she often did at the Backwoods Girls.

"No. What are they for?"

"What do you think they're for, dummy?" and she let the long peach-pink legs swing in the air.

"Ooh, how nice. What's this?"

"That's a garter belt," and Maggie dangled the pink rubber buttons in front of the five pairs of wondering eyes.

"Ooh, how wonderful. What's a garter belt?"

"It's what rich people like me wear to hold up their stockings. Look how the garters work."

"Ooh, lovely. What's this?"

"This is a closet."

"Ooh, what's a closet?"

"It's a place to keep clothes. Look. Look at all the clothes I have."

"Ooh," the Backwoods Girls cried out. They were crowded around the row of dresses hanging one beside another on the pole. "How beautiful."

Maggie lifted out the dress of brown wool and held it against her body. "Look how lovely it is," she said. "It was made just for me by a special dressmaker. Here, I'll show you how the buttons work."

"Ooh," they cried. "May I try it on? May *I*? May *I*? May *I*?"

"No," Maggie said, putting it back in the closet. "You're too skinny for it. It was made for someone better nourished than you," and she began now to unpack her duffel bag, transferring her frayed underwear, her torn socks, and her sweater with the enlarged buttonholes and thin elbows to the dresser drawers.

"Ooh, what's this?" they asked as Maggie came to her bitten ball-point pen.

"That's a pen," and Maggie laid it on the writing table in the corner. "Look what happens when I move the point across this paper. See? It makes writing. It's magic. I can make pictures with it—look, here's a picture of you," and she drew five circles with sticks for mouths and O's for eyes. "And it writes names. See? That says 'Maggie.'"

"Ooh, how wonderful! Write my name, too. Write mine, write mine, write mine."

"All right, but don't shout. I'll write all your names. This is Mary. This is Kate. Elizabeth. Helen. Anne."

She conducted them now—five barefoot girls with tattered dresses on their bodies and wonder in their eyes—around the room. "This is a sink. Look. See this silver handle? It's called a faucet. Look what happens when I turn it." A spurt of orange liquid burst from the tiny spout, coughed down the drain, and then turned clear.

"Ooh, how wonderful. What's this?"

"That's a mirror."

"Oh, a mirror. Ooh, look. There's another room inside. And another Maggie. Look. How wonderful!"

"No, dummies. That's just a piece of glass. See?" and she rapped it with her knuckles.

"Ooh, what's this? It's a little arm. Someone is under the bed. It's a little person."

"That isn't a little person, stupid," Maggie answered. "That's a doll," and she pulled out the pink rubber body from behind the bedspread.

"Ooh, a doll. What's a doll?"

"It's something you play with. You pretend it's a real baby and you take its clothes off. Like this," and she lifted the little pink dress, as Aunt Lillian had done, so that the Backwoods Girls could examine the white underwear with its careful ruffles and tight elastic.

"Ooh, how wonderful. Show us more."

Maggie couldn't remember when she had last held a doll,

and the body in her hand now felt strangely light and soft. "Look how it moves its head back and forth," she said, "and its arms. And look. Its shoes and socks come off, too, and you can get it all undressed and give it a bath and stuff." By now she had taken all the doll's clothes off and arranged them in a row on her bed. The naked doll still lay in her hands, soft and smooth. "Listen," she whispered, and very slowly she pushed in its stomach so that it let out its small cry.

"Ooh," the Backwoods Girls cried out in alarm. "It's hurt!"

"No," Maggie said. "It's hungry. It wants its bottle." She looked around the room and finally seized her ball-point pen. "Here," she said. "Look how it drinks," and she put the pen point into the doll's mouth.

"Ooh, let me try. Let me, let me, let me."

"No," Maggie said. "And don't shout. You'll make her cry again," and for a long while she held the doll in her hands, feeding it from her pen. "Now she wants to go to sleep," she said, dressing it again. "No, she doesn't. She wants to cry. Listen. Listen to her howl," and she pressed the soft rubber bulge under the doll's pink dress over and over until the cries became a rhythmic wail.

"Ooh," the Backwoods Girls said, "she really is hurt. Listen to her holler. Make her stop, make her stop."

"No," said Maggie, "dolls are dumb," and she pressed

the doll's stomach some more, but she finally stopped, dropping the doll to the floor.

"Ooh, what's this?" Maggie and the Backwoods Girls were at the closed door now.

"It's a door. Look what happens when I turn the knob."

Maggie stared into the long, dark hall with its row of doors, heavy and closed, on either side. Nine closed doors. What lay behind them? Beds, like hers, with white spreads and navy blankets folded across the feet? Closets with rows of brown dresses and dresser drawers with long brown stockings and pink garter belts? Unknown girls at the mirror over an orange-stained sink, combing and combing their hair?

She led the five wondering girls along the walls. The building was totally still, and she walked softly, groping for the little oval light pulls that had lit their way when Aunt Lillian had led her to her room. She rested her ear for a moment against the first door, but there was no sound, and she turned the handle.

CHAPTER SIX

A massive bed stood in the center of the room. A massive bed with heavy carvings and a large wooden knob at each corner. Maggie approached it cautiously and slid her hand over one of the knobs; it was smooth as a glass ball and as cold. A headmistress's room, with a braided rug on the floor, framed scenes of some foreign city with canals and strange boats, and a dresser cluttered with bottles and hair things.

"This is a bedroom," she said in her head to her five girls. "And this is a dresser. And these"—she held up a clutch of pink objects—"are curlers."

"Ooh, what are curlers?"

"You wrap your hair around them and after a while you

have a whole bunch of curls. Look, I'll show you," and she slowly wound ropes of her hair, wet still from her mouth, around the fat tubes in her hand, clamping them shut with a little click.

"Ooh, how wonderful. What beautiful curls. All pink."

"No, dummies, *these* aren't the curls. Later, when I take the curlers out, you'll see. I'll have beautiful curls all around my face."

"Ooh, lovely. What's this?"

"That's a necklace. See this red stone? It's a real ruby. It's precious." Maggie cupped her hand and let the gold chain sink into a tiny heap, like a hill of sand, over the red jewel in her palm, burying it. "See this tiny circle?" she said, pointing with her fingernail. "That's the clasp, and this is how you fasten it around your neck. See how beautiful it makes me look? Only rich people have necklaces. Like me." She stared at herself in the large mirror on the wall and turned one way and another until the stone at her throat caught the light and shone like a drop of crimson dew. "See how it sparkles?"

"Ooh, what's this?"

"That's a bunch of keys."

"Ooh, what's keys?"

"Keys are for unlocking doors. Look," and she led them to the bedroom door where she tried one key after another until she found one that turned. "Ooh, look what happens," the girls all cried as a little metal tongue shot in and out of its plate.

"Come on," Maggie said. "Let's see the other rooms," and she led the five Backwoods Girls from the bedroom and down the hall.

"Let's see what's in here," she said, opening another door and stepping into a room not unlike the one she had just left. The other aunt's bedroom. Which one? Green or brown? Freckles or wrinkles? Harriet or Lillian? It didn't much matter.

"Ooh, look how big."

"Yes, it's big. Look what happens when I pull this string—the curtains open! And when I pull it again they close. Now they open. Now they close. It's magic. Watch. Open. Close."

"Ooh, you broke the string."

"Right. I can break anything I want around here."

"Ooh, that's bad."

"No, it's not. It's good. Look at this. It's perfume. Smell," and she sprayed a puff of mist into the air.

"Ooh, delicious. Spray some on me, and on me, and on me."

"Okay, line up. You first, Anne," and she pressed the little rubber bulb five times more. "Now look at these. These are evening slippers. They're for going to parties."

"Ooh, how shiny."

"They're satin. Silver satin," and she rubbed their smooth

skin against her thumb, her cheek, her upper lip. "Look how tall they make me."

"Ooh, how wonderful. May we wear them too?"

"No, you're too poor. Anyway, you'd fall. The heels are too high for you," and she extended her arms to balance her way out of the room and across the hall to another door.

"Ooh, what room is this?"

"This is the bathroom, dummies. See the tub?"

"Ooh, what's a tub?"

"This. It's like the sink I showed you before, only you get into it all the way. Watch," and she turned the taps on full force. "Here's how you take a bath." She removed the silver slippers and her socks and put both feet into the steamy bubbles. "It makes you clean," she said, stepping out again. "And this is what you use for drying yourself. It's called a towel, and you rub it back and forth like this until your feet are dry."

"Ooh, how wonderful," and the five Backwoods Girls waited while Maggie slipped her feet into the silver shoes again.

"Now follow me," and she led them down the hall to another silent door. This one opened to a bedroom just like hers, with a white metal bed, a dark blanket folded across its lower end, a sink, a dresser, a writing desk, a closet.

She closed the door and continued down the hall, the five wondering girls, silent now and almost forgotten, trailing behind. The next five doors opened onto the same kind of room, quiet and still. At the fifth room Maggie walked over to the dresser and pulled open the drawers. They were all empty, and the closet, too, its door tugged open, stood hushed and dark. Where *was* everyone?

Sometimes on the day of a new arrival the girls in a boarding school would play a mean trick. They would hide in a closet or a storeroom, all of them, piled into a tiny space so that they could barely breathe, while a strange hush would fall over the halls; and then in a burst of screams they would wildly jump out as the new girl passed by. Maggie had been asked once to join a group that had planned to do just that, but she had remained instead in her room, listening to the solitary footsteps of the new arrival—Mary Louise her name was—and jumping in fright herself when the burst of screams finally broke through the silence in the halls.

Maybe the girls in this school were planning to play the same trick on her. Maybe they were all squeezed into some dark closet, listening to one another breathe, listening to the heels of the silver satin slippers on her feet draw closer and closer, waiting for her shadow to darken the keyhole, when they would spring out and envelop her in their screams.

But she would be prepared. She wouldn't jump or turn when the door—which one would it be?—was finally flung open, and she would continue down the hall, not looking to the left or to the right, not showing, even, that she had heard. Still, she felt hidden ears straining for the sound of her footfall, and hidden eyes, too, perhaps, searching through some unknown crack.

"Ooh, what's this?" the Backwoods Girls asked. They had reached the end of the hall and were standing in front of the last door, bigger than the rest and paneled in wood so dark it looked black.

"This is another door," Maggie explained to the Backwoods Girls, and she cautiously put her ear against it for the sounds of breathing or a giggle muffled by a hand. "It's a big door," she went on, hearing nothing and turning the handle. Surprisingly, she found herself not in another room but at the bottom of a short flight of steps ending in still another door.

Maggie listened at the frame of this one, too, and then turned the knob. The schoolroom. Carefully she stepped inside. The desks, rows and rows of them, were of the kind she had seen in books of long ago. They were attached, one to another, in a kind of endlessness that made her, closing her eyes, feel quietly dizzy. The seat back of one became the front of the next, and the seat back of *that* formed the front of still another, and on and on, as though in a bad dream, although they did have an end, of course, and a beginning. The very first desk in the row had no seat in front of it at all. Just a back.

Another door, narrow this time and painted white, stood

in the center of the opposite wall, and Maggie led the five barefoot girls across the room so she could open it. She turned the knob and then held still. A bare room. The Backwoods Girls asked no questions as she gazed into the sunlight pouring unchecked through the narrow windows. A bare room, and yet everything about it suggested the presence of someone suddenly gone. A darkened rectangle of floor varnish outlined a rug now removed, and at the center of each wall hung a hook that held no picture. Wooden rods from which no curtain hung rested above each window frame, and a row of discolored circles marked the places where flowerpots had once stood on the sills. The window looked onto the same garden she had seen from her own room, but now she noticed a swing—a single wooden board hanging by ropes from the branch of a tree. A breeze had stirred it slightly, and it gave a crooked start, once, twice, the only moving object in a frozen scene. Maggie turned away.

In this room, too, there was a single door in the opposite wall. Did this house have no end? Was every room going to contain a door leading to another room in a chain as dizzying as the thought of the seats and desks in the schoolroom? But this door opened only onto an empty closet. A single hanger swayed on the pole, and a strange silence swept over her like a hushed wind.

CHAPTER SEVEN

❦

"Come on," she said, while at the very edge of her vision the swing in the garden continued to sway on its distant tree. "Come on," she said in her head to the Backwoods Girls, and she led them from the empty room, through the schoolroom with its desks bolted to the floor, along the hallway with its rows of closed doors, down the stairs, and into the front hall.

"Look," she said, lifting a green velvet hat from an arm of the mirrored clothes rack and pulling it over the curlers in her hair. "See how lovely I am?" and she turned her face from side to side in the mirror.

"Ooh, lovely," they all answered. "And look. There's another lovely person, with a hat just like yours."

"Yes, another person. And look. She does what I tell her to. Go away!" she ordered into the mirror, and the image disappeared as Maggie conducted the five girls with their dirty, inquiring little faces along a hall, through a door, and into a blaze of light—the garden.

Ooh, how wonderful, she almost said herself as she glimpsed for the first time the proportions of the grounds behind the building.

Less a garden than a meadow, it stretched far into the distance, with clumps of trees here and there, occasional flower beds blazing with the reds and yellows of September, and, far off to the right, a stand of white trees casting lacy shadows on the grass. It was a good garden, she decided. Better than most.

She stepped cautiously out into the sun, turning once to glance at the building behind her, to catch sight, maybe, of a vanishing face, but the windows were blank and the wall silent. The garden, too, was still; the immense lawn, from the doorway where she stood to the distant rim of woods, was quiet, and only the swing, empty and lifeless, stirred in the breeze.

"What's that?" the Backwoods Girls asked as Maggie picked through the damp grass in her silver shoes.

"That's a swing," she answered. "You sit on it and push your feet back and forth and you go higher and higher in the air. Come on, I'll show you how. First you, Kate," and she gave the swing a heavy push. "Put your feet up when you go forward and down when you go back. Now you, Elizabeth." In the next moment, something snapped, tore, pulled away, and the wooden seat danced crazily from one rope. The other had broken and it twitched now in the dust like a dying snake.

"Ooh," the girls all said. "What happened?"

"It broke," Maggie answered. "It doesn't matter. It was a dumb swing. And now," she added, leading them all away, "look at these. These are roses. And these . . ." She paused.

They had come to the group of white trees Maggie had seen from the doorway, and she felt strangely drawn to them, as though they had been set aside for her as a private room. She knew their name, and she had the little girls ask, "What are these?" so she could answer, "Birches." And she went on, "But no one is allowed near them except me. They're my private trees and you can't come near. Anyway, you're too stupid and dirty to be here." She was tiring of their company, and she wanted to be all alone so she could enter the shade of the white trees that seemed only hers. "Go away now," she commanded, and in an instant the five little girls returned to their home in the backwoods where they would wait until she had something else to display before their wondering eyes.

The air was cool and the wind penetrated the sleeves of her blouse, but she left the small warmth of the sun on the lawn and sought the shadows of the birch branches that crossed and recrossed one another on the ground, enfolding her like some giant web. She imagined herself to be a spider, following with the toes of her silver slippers every woven thread until she grew dizzy, and she sat down between two trunks of pocked white bark.

It was nice being among the trees. It was like having a house of your own. Idly, she gathered some long sticks and laid them end to end to mark off separate rooms on the grass. The bedroom would be over here, against this tree; the kitchen, here. This would be the living room, where she was sitting; this rock could be the table and the little mossy mound over there could be the chair. The grass could be the rug. . . .

All at once a door slammed shut somewhere and a cry went up: "There she is!" and in an instant the shadow ribbons on Maggie's arms and legs were invaded by a spread of new shadows—massive heads, arms, bodies, legs—and four hands were upon her, pulling her to her feet and dragging her across the lawn, back to the school building.

"That's my hat!" one aunt was crying.

"Take those curlers out of your hair!" the other shouted.

"She smells of perfume!"

"She's got my necklace on! Look! She's stolen my necklace!"

"Look at my evening shoes! They're all wet! What are you doing with my evening shoes? Take off my shoes! Take them off! You're ruining them! Look at those feet in my shoes!"

"The upstairs is a shambles!"

"She left water running in the tub! She muddied up the towels! She tracked up the upstairs hall! She broke the window curtain pull! She threw the keys on the bathroom floor! And left the doors all open!"

"Even *their* door."

"And after we gave her all those clothes."

"And the doll. After I bought her that doll."

"She's a disgusting child."

"Disgusting."

"Enchanting."

Maggie looked up quickly at this new tone in the storm of anger surrounding her.

"Absolutely enchanting."

Uncle Morris was standing in the doorway. "Stop!" he commanded, and she didn't know whether he was directing his order to her or to her aunts. "Stop right where I can see you. Good. I want to admire the effect. Step a little to the left now. Ah, perfect," he said. "Perfect. A silver slipper on her foot, a ruby at her throat."

Maggie stole a look at the necklace with its single red

stone (was it *really* a ruby?) and at the evening slippers on her feet. The satin was darkened now with water and streaked green with grass juice.

"And blossoms to her hair," Uncle Morris continued.

"Be still, Morris." It was Aunt Lillian speaking now. "She's stolen Harriet's necklace and ruined my best shoes and destroyed half the house, and you stand there reciting poetry."

It did sound like poetry, a little, and Maggie wondered if someone had really written a poem about a girl who looked just as she did now with a ruby bead at her throat and silver slippers on her feet. And blossoms—what were the blossoms? Oh, the curlers. The pink curlers. And blossoms to her hair.

"It was a mistake to bring her here. I told you, Morris, that it would be a mistake."

"Take her back to her room," Aunt Harriet said. Fingers were at the back of her shoulders now and she shrank away, but someone was holding her still as the hat was taken from her head, the curlers tugged from her hair, the slippers pulled from her feet, and the tiny gold clasp at the back of her neck unlocked. Maggie was glad that the other girls in the school were not in sight. They would remember a scene like this and remind her of it later on. They would think up a name that would sting her with its memory; and among themselves, but within her hearing, they would talk about this moment when all the things she had put on were torn from her body at once.

"It was a mistake bringing *any* child here after so many years," Aunt Lillian was saying. "But this one is the worst. I knew the moment I set eyes on her she'd be impossible to handle."

"Impossible," Aunt Harriet agreed. "It was a mistake to consider it."

"Impossible to handle," Aunt Lillian repeated. "She should have been sent to some boarding school, with trained supervisors to look after her."

"We're too old to take on such a burden ourselves."

Maggie stared at them. She should have been sent to a boarding school? Then what was *this?* And she looked from one face to the other until she understood at last that this was not a boarding school after all. There were no other girls here. The dormitory rooms upstairs were bare and their closets empty because no one lived in them. This was the house she had been promised all along—this great stone building!—and she would live in it with no one but her two aunts and her uncle—and the Backwoods Girls, who spoke only silently, in her head.

CHAPTER EIGHT

❧❦❧

"She should have been sent to some boarding school," Aunt Lillian had said. "She's impossible to handle."

To *handle*? Handle was what you did to the smooth knob on the bedpost when you slipped your palm across it. Handle was what you did to the china lace skirt on the ballerina in the curio cabinet, to the gold chain necklace with its single red stone, to the silver satin slippers standing side by side on the closet floor. Was she impossible to handle? Experimentally she ran her fingers along her cheek as though it were the smooth satin skin of a silver slipper, and let a rope of her wet brown hair collect in her cupped hand like a chain of golden links. She squeezed her forearm as though it were the rubber limb of a doll, and, with her thumb, whitened sections of the pale-blue vein that ran like a river from her wrist to her elbow. Was she impossible to handle?

But of course her aunt didn't mean "handle" like that at all. She meant Maggie was impossible to control. She meant Maggie was fresh, nasty, mean, disobedient, willful, rebellious, thieving—all those things she had been called by people who had to look after her. She meant that within an hour somebody was going to come up to Maggie's room and tell her to pack her things because she would have to leave.

Where would they send her? That was probably what they were deciding right now. At this very moment, while Maggie pressed the vein in her arm, watching it whiten and darken in turn, her two aunts and her uncle were downstairs deciding among themselves where she should next be sent. "There are places for children like you," one headmistress had warned her. "Kids' jail" is what other children called such places. "Maggie's going to kids' jail." Is that where her aunts and her uncle would send her now? Kids' jail?

She put a strand of hair in her mouth and reached into the drawer of the little writing table, extracting from it her battered deck of cards, gray, sticky, and uneven in their stretched-out rubber band. One by one she laid them out on her bed.

Solitaire was the only card game she played. Some roommate had once taught her how. "It's a game you play all by yourself," the girl had explained, and Maggie had stood by and watched in growing fascination as the rows of cards were counted out, faceup and facedown, on that faraway dormitory floor. One two three four five six seven. One two three four five six. One two three four five. One two three four. The patterns were wonderful: red on black, black on red, red black red black red, and as soon as she had mastered the rules she had played it all the rest of that distant afternoon, alone in her room. Soon it became her principal pastime, and when she closed her eyes at night, double-torsoed kings, queens, and jacks would file in solemn procession in the darkness behind her lids, their families of tens and nines, eights and sevens, black red black red, all marching in tight order close behind.

Now the cards were dealt out across the bedspread, and she paused to listen for the voices of her aunts and uncle planning her future from somewhere downstairs, in the parlor, maybe, or around that long dining table. Noiselessly she went to the door and opened it an inch. The hallway was a long dark tunnel, thick with silence. No board creaked, no whisper came, and Maggie closed the door again, returning to the silent cards, the silent walls, the silent bed.

If this place wasn't a boarding school, then why was there a plaque on the front entrance saying it was? And who had slept in all these rooms with their boarding school beds and writing desks? Who, for that matter, had used the schoolroom? What *was* this place, anyway?

Red black red black red black. "These are cards," she explained to the Backwoods Girls, who had suddenly appeared at her bedside. "Here, I'll tell you their names. This one is called Queen of Hearts and this one is Ace of Diamonds."

"Ooh, how wonderful," they all said. "How do you remember them all?"

"It's easy," Maggie answered. "I can remember anything," and she continued laying out the cards, red on black, black on red. "Look, here's how to play."

Kids' jail, she thought. What were those places like? Gray and old, probably, like the building she was in now, and filled with children like her, all impossible to handle, all crowded into tiny rooms—cells—and all watched from morning until night by women in white uniforms. Matrons.

The light entering the window was fading now, and she squinted at the pale kings and queens lined up on the bed. It was growing late, and no one had come up to tell her to pack her things. Maybe, instead of sending her away, her aunts would simply punish her. How? she wondered. You could always size up a headmistress by the way she punished. The ones who knew what they were about and weren't afraid of you gave you a stinging slap across your face and called you some sort of name. Brat, usually. The others, the ones who were afraid you would get the better of them, shouted all over the place and sent you to your room, or made you miss recess for a week—or desserts or television or whatever everyone else could have. It never much mattered to Maggie. She hated recess, everybody always crowded around the television screen so she couldn't see it anyway, and the desserts were usually pudding.

The worst kind of headmistress was the one who didn't punish at all. Who didn't even get angry. "Maggie isn't feeling cooperative today," she would explain in a pleasant voice to someone whose knees you had just kicked in. Then she would take you to her office and make you sit next to her while she told you how wonderful you were and how much you'd grown. Not grown *taller.* More *mature.* "You've become much more mature, Maggie, and we are all proud of your development." Then there'd be a lecture on how even though Maggie had grown so mature she still had to work on expressing her anger in more constructive ways. But Maggie wouldn't be listening. Instead, she'd be staring at the leather appointment book on the desk and figuring out a way to slide it under her arm and out the door. For a diary. She could write things in a diary and somehow keep the days from being lost, one after another. She could tell what she had done each hour: Seven A.M.: Got up. Brushed teeth. Got dressed.

It was growing late. There was no color left at all in the garden, and a star appeared just above the crown of birch branches. Suddenly there was a rustle at her door and Maggie froze. They were coming for her at last. They had made up their minds and now she would be told to pack her things. She slid off the bed. A small shower of cards slid off with her, coming to rest, like silent leaves from a shaken branch, against her feet. She faced the door, waiting for the knob to turn or the frame to quiver at a knock, but she heard only the clatter of something being settled on the floor and then quick, retreating footsteps. When the hall was silent again, she opened the door a crack and stared down at a supper tray—a bowl of soup, a sandwich, and a glass of milk, its rim of bubbles not yet broken. Carefully she closed the door on it and returned to her bed.

"This," she said to the Backwoods Girls, "is a bed."

"Ooh, what's a bed?"

"It's to sleep on, dummies. I don't sleep on the floor, the way you do. I have a bed all to myself. I have this whole room to myself, in fact. Everything in it is mine to keep for as long as I like," and she closed the curtains, so that no light at all entered the room that she now knew would be hers for what might be a long while.

CHAPTER NINE

Whenever Maggie looked back upon her first full morning at Adelphi Hills, she would think only of its profound silence. So quiet was the house, so still, she felt as though it had been frozen into a painting, and for a long time she couldn't tell whether it was too early for anyone to be awake or too late for anyone still to be at home. At last she rose and parted the curtains. It was barely morning; the garden was whitened with pale dew, and the birches where she had laid out her little rooms with sticks the day before hung like slender ghosts against a gray sky.

How would she be awakened here? she wondered. In some places there would be a clangorous bell; in others a house mother would snap the window shades up, letting the glare of the day attack your eyes. But there was no bell or house mother here, and the two aunts who found her impossible to handle might decide not to awaken her at all. The tray that had been left outside her door the night before had been removed. Maggie had heard it being lifted from the floor, and she had heard, too, the rustle of a dress and the sound of footsteps disappearing down the hall.

She sat on the window seat a long time, watching the color seep back into the lawn and wondering what it was going to be like to live in a boarding school, or whatever this was, with no other children. Often, walking about among the halls and grounds of her old schools, she had pretended that the buildings had been emptied of everyone but herself, and she had suddenly become their sole inhabitant. This big room will be my bedroom, she had decided, and the auditorium will be a ballroom where I will dance alone. It will have red wallpaper and a black rug, and there will be white curtains on all the windows. Those were her favorite colors: red and black and white, the colors of her playing cards. The best part was always the garden. Usually she would let it remain unchanged—the concrete playing field and the groups of trees would stay as they were. The only difference would be that no one else would be there, and she would aim basketballs at the hoop and wind about among the trees totally, totally alone, her whole life through.

Now she had an enormous house almost to herself, and she wondered what it would be like.

Silently she got dressed, not in any of the dresses hanging ghostlike from the pole in the closet, but in her own clothes—a thin skirt, too cool for a late September day, a tan blouse with a split in the underarm seam, and unmatched socks—and slowly made her way along the hall and down the stairs.

The gray morning light was beginning to creep through the parlor curtains and settle on the gray of the walls, leaving no glow. The first thing Maggie saw was the pair of portraits above the mantel, and she gazed up at the two austere faces, noticing today something she had missed the day before—a small black-and-white dog curled at the man's feet. Maggie put her hand out.

"Don't touch!" a voice cried, and Maggie spun around. Her two great-aunts were seated side by side, quiet as cats, on the gray plush sofa. Their bodies were erect, their hands folded in their laps, and their eyes fastened intently upon her. They were wearing different colors today, and Maggie had to squint in the gray light to find the freckles that would distinguish one from the other.

"Paintings are to be admired by the eye, not the hand," one of them said: Aunt Harriet—wrinkles, no freckles. "That is a rule. Remember it at all times." Maggie turned back to the pictures, her hands at her sides now, and examined the dog curled sleepily at the feet of its master.

"Look at your aunt when she speaks to you." That was the other one—Aunt Lillian, freckles. "And don't squint. Squinting weakens the muscles of the eye."

Maggie faced her two aunts again, looking from one to the other and finally dropping her eyes to the rug with its vines and blossoms still colorless in the early light.

Aunt Harriet suddenly spoke out. "Those were the founders of the Academy," she explained. "This building at one time housed a girls' school, and it was founded by the two people whose portraits you see. The Greens."

"They were our ancestors," Aunt Lillian put in. "They are your ancestors as well," she added, running her eye over Maggie's body, "although I can't say they would be happy to know it."

Her ancestors! Maggie jumped at the thought, and her eye shot back to the two faces in their sturdy frames. Imagine having ancestors when she didn't even have a mother and a father.

"Now we are the only ones left," Aunt Lillian continued. "We and your uncle Morris. And you, of course," she added with a sigh.

Uncle Morris. Where *was* Uncle Morris? She realized now that of all the rooms she had entered the day before, none seemed to belong to him. Where did he sleep?

"The Academy was founded as a school for carefully chosen girls," Aunt Lillian went on. "Girls with character. Character is the most important element in a human being's life. Remember that at all times. The founders cared a great deal about character."

"Character and healthful living," Aunt Harriet said. "Stop sucking your hair. That's a disgusting habit. Disgusting."

"They ran the school for nearly fifty years, and it was thought to be one of the finest in the country."

"Then came the misfortune, and—"

"Now the new Academy is down the road," Aunt Lillian interrupted, "and it is run by people who take any children at all."

"They take children of wealth," Aunt Harriet said. "Wealth and character do not always agree."

"They take boys," Aunt Lillian said.

"They will take you," Aunt Harriet told Maggie. "Tomorrow you will begin attending New Adelphi Hills Academy. It is not at all like the original, but nothing else is available, and you will receive a small amount of learning there. As for your character, we will look after that ourselves."

School. Tomorrow she would have to go to school. A day school, where everybody went home every afternoon instead of just on weekends or not at all. A rich kids' school. Her stomach sank.

"Stand up straight," Aunt Harriet said. "A healthy body requires a straight spine. Say that to yourself several times a day: A healthy body requires a straight spine."

"And change your clothes," Aunt Lillian added. "You're having a visitor today."

A visitor? Maggie's spine stiffened of its own accord, and she stepped back into the quiet gaze of the man and woman in black and white over the mantel. What visitor? In the past a visitor had meant a doctor who pried open your clenched teeth with a slab of wood, or a psychologist who asked you to draw a picture of a family and then remained silent when you scribbled a parade of tiny spiders along the bottom of the paper.

"We have invited a friend for you," Aunt Lillian explained. "She is the granddaughter of an acquaintance of ours and her name is Jeanette."

A friend! "I don't want a friend."

"Everyone wants a friend," Aunt Lillian answered. "'Happy is the house that shelters a friend.' Ralph Waldo Emerson wrote that. You must read Ralph Waldo Emerson. He will improve your character."

Maggie withdrew her hair from her mouth and painted little circles on her cheek with its sharpened point. "I don't want a friend," she repeated, backing against the wall.

"Jeanette is a wholesome child. You need wholesome companions. She is also an accomplished singer. She has the voice of a lark. If you ask her she will sing for you."

"I don't want a lark—a friend. I don't want a friend."

Jeanette wore her hair in a single heavy braid clasped at top and bottom with purple beads. Her eyes were wide set and brown, and around her wrist she wore a silver chain with a slim oval plate that Maggie knew, without looking, bore the engraving of her name. All the girls at her other schools—the girls with families, not the charity girls like her— had them.

Jeanette crossed the room toward her and unexpectedly extended her hand. Maggie had never before shaken hands with anyone, and she remained frozen on the rug. After a long moment, Jeanette pulled Maggie's hand from behind her back and gave it a vicious squeeze. "How do you do?" she said, and she took a seat next to the window, where she crossed and recrossed her ankles with their straight white socks, evenly matched.

Maggie sat against the opposite wall and riffled the pages of a copy of *National Geographic*, glancing at the pictures. Birds, mostly. She lifted one page to her face and squinted at it with extreme care. Jeanette leaned over and measured the height of one sock against the other. Then she ran her fingernail along the wall, making Maggie's skin freeze. At last she spoke. "Do you like actors and actresses?"

Maggie didn't look up. "I don't go to the movies."

"I mean the game."

Maggie turned three more pages and came face to face

with an owl. "I don't play any games," she said eventually. "I'm too old for games."

"I'm older than you. And anyway, it's not the kind of game you play with pieces or anything. It's a talking game. First I think of an actor, say, and I give you his initials and you try to guess who it is. If you guess right, it's your turn. Otherwise I go again. You want to play?"

"No."

Jeanette fell silent and began exploring the room with her eyes. "What's that?" she finally asked, pausing at the curio cabinet. Maggie turned the page: an ad for T-shirts with pictures of endangered animals printed across their chests. A whale. A whooping crane. "What?" she asked, not looking up.

"In that cabinet."

Maggie glanced at the china ballerina balancing on one toe, and once again longed to run her finger along the edge of its brittle skirt. "That's mine," she said. "It's a dancer. It's all made of china. Even the skirt."

"No, I mean the elephants. On the other shelf."

Maggie shrugged. "I don't know. They're elephants."

"They look creepy. This whole house is creepy. How come everything is so dark in here? Everybody says this place is haunted. My brother told me not to come. He said they used to have a boarding school or something here and then something happened and it's been haunted ever since. Nobody wants to come here. Except your uncle, and even he doesn't want to come here. My brother says your uncle's crazy."

Maggie slowly tore off a piece of her thumbnail and put it in her mouth. Then Uncle Morris didn't live here. He only visited. Where *did* he live? She turned back to her magazine and the room fell silent again.

"Who are those?" Jeanette asked after a while.

Maggie turned another page. "Who?" she asked, not looking up.

"In those pictures."

Maggie glanced briefly at the two faces in the paintings. "I don't know," she said. "Ancestors." She returned to her bird pictures. "They're dead." She removed the softened thumbnail from her mouth and dropped it to the floor.

"You want to do something?" Jeanette's voice broke through the silence. "You want to play a game or what? You want to play ghost?"

Maggie jumped slightly. "What?"

"Ghost."

Maggie turned another page. "There's no such thing," she said.

"No, the word game, dummy. Don't you even know how to play ghost?"

"No."

"You spell out words," Jeanette said. "First I say a letter and then you say a letter, and you keep on going until you spell a word. Then if the word ends on you, you get G for ghost. And the first person who gets G-H-O-S-T is out. Suppose I say B. Now you say a letter."

Maggie studied a picture of an island filled with black-and-white birds with triangular red bills.

"Say a *letter*," Jeanette insisted.

"P," Maggie finally said.

"P?"

"Mmm."

"What word is that supposed to be?"

"Puffin. It's a bird."

"But I already said 'B'!"

"So?"

"So there's no word that begins B-P. You get G for ghost. You're one fifth of a ghost."

"There's no such thing."

Jeanette inserted a finger into her sock and slowly scratched the back of her heel. "You know why I don't go to the same school as you?" she asked. "Because I go to a performing arts school. I'm training to be a concert singer and I'm going to go on tour and stuff. I study voice. Voice is what you study when you're going to be a singer."

The tone of her voice was familiar, and Maggie recognized it as the one she used when she addressed her five little girls from the backwoods. "That's a lie," she said.

There was silence in the room for a long moment, and then Jeanette suddenly burst out, "I know all about you. My grandmother told me. She told me your mother and father were killed in a car crash or something and you've been thrown out of a whole bunch of boarding schools and foster homes and finally your aunts took you because no one else wanted you and they had to because they're relatives."

Maggie flipped the pages of the magazine quickly and stopped suddenly at a glossy study of a brown-and-gray bird. It had speckles on its creamy breast, and it resembled a sparrow more than anything else, but in flight it took command of the entire page, and the trees in the distance were small and vague beneath the spread of its wings. It was a lark, the caption said, an Old World lark, and she could see by its open beak that it was in full song. In a moment she had ripped the page in half and then in half again, so that she had four fluttering strips of broken wings and fragmented feathers. These she crushed into a solid ball, and walking, almost marching—step-stop, step-stop—across the room, she reached Jeanette's frozen figure and in a quick movement pressed the crumpled bird hard against her mouth. A soft cry rose, like the cry of the rubber doll when Maggie had pressed its face in the day before, and Jeanette's face flamed.

"I think you're rotten," Jeanette whispered, pulling the

pieces of paper from her lips. "You're rotten," she said. "You're the rottenest person I've ever met. I'm glad your mother and father are dead. I'd feel sorry for them having to live with you." She began moving away now. "I'm glad you have to live in this creepy house with your aunts." A few bits of paper still clung to her mouth, and Maggie saw part of a beak on one tooth and, on another, a piece of wing. "And you can't hurt me by staring at me like that either. I don't have to look at you at all. I don't have to look at you ever again, in fact. I don't have to come back here. I only came because my grandmother made me, and I'm never coming again. Never, never, never."

Aunt Harriet and Aunt Lillian were suddenly standing at the parlor door, and the two girls sprang apart. "What's happening here?" one of them asked. "What's that all over the floor?"

"It's a game," Maggie answered quickly.

"A game! What sort of a game is it that requires you to strew paper all over the rug?"

Maggie picked up some of the shreds from the floor. "Ghost," she answered, throwing the torn bits of wings and beak into the fireplace beneath the two portraits with their pale faces and distant eyes.

CHAPTER TEN

❦

Maggie stood alone in the corridor outside the sixth-grade classroom of New Adelphi Hills Academy and ran her eye along the row of labels over the coat hooks on the wall. Alyssa. Barbara. Gregory. Sharon. Catherine P. Robert. Howard. Catherine M. Carolyn. Edwin. Randi, with an *i*. Diana. Her new classmates. She looked at their jackets, all puffed with thick stuffing and all stitched with little emblems from ski resorts. Alyssa's was green, and at an opening in a seam a tiny feather stuck through. Beneath it, side by side, stood two perfect leather boots with carved designs. Above hung a striped stocking hat with an enormous pompon. The weather had turned suddenly cold and damp, and winter clothes had been brought out, for the first time in the season probably:

The corridor smelled of camphor and musty closets. Carolyn's hook also held a long yellow scarf, with foot-long fringes.

All the girls had the same kind of hat. *All* of them. Long wool pull-ons with huge pompons, some green and blue, some red and black, one—the nicest—violet and lemon. They hung one beside the other like a string of pennants on a ship. Maggie lifted the violet-and-lemon one from its hook and pulled it over her head, swinging it around so that the pompon banged against her ears and then dragged on the floor like an elephant's trunk.

Inside, the teacher was explaining Maggie's "situation" to the boys and girls in her class. There hadn't been time to warn them that there would be a new girl arriving that day. Maggie had been brought to school at the wrong hour, and so she was asked to wait in the hall while everybody was given the lecture teachers always gave about being kind to newcomers, especially when they were like Maggie.

She ran her foot along the floor molding and gazed at the row of clothing spread across the wall: hat, jacket, and boots for Alyssa; hat, jacket, and boots for Barbara. Jacket, no hat, no boots for Gregory. Just like paper-doll outfits, and Maggie thought now of the little paper dresses and coats, each with a name imprinted on a shoulder tab, that her old roommates would attach to little cardboard boys and girls in monogrammed underwear lined up along the windowsill.

What would they be like, she wondered, the real boys and girls who belonged to these hats and jackets on the wall? Slowly, in her mind, she gave each outfit a body, filling in a face under each hat, a pair of hands below the sleeves, legs above the boots. Alyssa would have short curly hair that she would shake a lot and a smooth brown scab clinging like a polished beetle to each knee. Barbara would have a lovely wire band across her teeth and a thick braid that she would swing around like a rope. All the girls, in fact, would shake their hair a lot. Diana would have a fringe of bangs that she would sometimes shake and sometimes blow from the corners of her mouth, scattering it across her forehead like a row of startled hens. Robert would have a fat, buttery face and creased wrists, and Gregory would have a face like a rodent's and small, powerful fingers with which, in two weeks' time, he would twist Maggie's arm into vicious burns.

There were no extra coat hooks, Maggie noticed, and that meant that somebody would be asked to share with her. "Randi," the teacher would ask, "I know you won't mind sharing your coat hook with Maggie," and Randi with an *i* would remain silent. No, she wouldn't mind. She'd be *happy* to have her shiny, down-filled jacket with the embroidered ski patches make room for Maggie's brown wool coat with its misshapen sleeves and uneven hem. She would *love* to have her violet-and-lemon hat nestle next to Maggie's brown beret with its peeling leather band and torn school emblem.

Randi with an *i* would be Maggie's first enemy.

Little fragments of the teacher's voice were drifting into the hall, and Maggie tightened her ears against them. The speech was one she didn't care to hear. The teacher would be explaining to curly-haired Alyssa and rat-faced Gregory and butter-fat Robert and everyone else why it was necessary to be considerate and thoughtful of Maggie. "Maggie has had a great deal of trouble in her life," she would say. Teachers loved to tell about Maggie's trouble, especially the part about her mother and father. "Both her mother *and* her father have passed away." They always said "passed away." Then she'd start in on all the schools Maggie had been to, leaving out the part about how she'd been thrown out of each one. "Maggie has been to many schools with other customs and other rules, so she may appear a bit different at first." "Different" was another word teachers loved. "Maggie is a *different* child," when hateful was what they meant. Next would come the part about cooperating. "I know you are all eager to cooperate in making Maggie a happy member of the class." Happy member of the class. Then she'd get to the part about how they should all treat their newcomer as they would want to be treated themselves, and she'd use a whole lot of words like "ethical" and "understanding" and everyone would grow solemn.

And if Alyssa and Barbara and Sharon and the two Catherines and Carolyn and Diana were like the girls in all the other schools Maggie had ever been to, they *would* be nice to her—at first. Except for Randi, whose clothes would have to hang next to hers on the coat hook, they would all actually *like* being nice to her. They would treat her as though she were Mary Lennox from *The Secret Garden,* suddenly ushered into their midst and needing to be looked after. Girls always liked being nice to the new girl, especially if she had had "a great deal of trouble in her life."

They would even fight over who was to be her partner on the way to the lunchroom and who would show her the way to the bathroom. Outside, at recess, they'd all cluster around her and Alyssa would tell her how nice her clothes were—her brown school skirt with the glistening grease stain along the hem and her tan blouse with its split underarm seam—and one of the Catherines would pick her first when they were choosing up sides for a game.

It was always the worst part of going to a new school, the time when everybody tried to be nice, but it never lasted very long. In a few days or a week everybody would begin to hate her and be happy at last not to have to feel sorry for her anymore. Pretty soon, maybe in two weeks, she would stand alone on the playground where today she would be made first player on the team. Groups of girls would form— in the corridor, on the playground, in the lunchroom—and she would hear her own name—Maggie!—then a laugh, and silence. Someone would imitate her walk, and now and then she would catch sight of her name on a note passed across her desk to someone on her other side. Later they would grow bolder, and finally her clothes, the same clothes that they would admire today, would be inked up and her desk smeared with glue.

It was dark in the corridor. The walls were paneled from floor to ceiling in heavy wood. All the schools she had ever attended had at one time served some other purpose; this one, her aunts had told her, was a former country estate house. Never in her life had she sat in the normal sort of classroom she was always reading about in books: a large rectangular room with a row of gray steel lockers along one wall and, on another, ceiling-high windows that had to be opened and closed with a pole. She had never known anything but irregular rooms with bricked-up fireplaces, window seats, alcoves, linen closets, and, once, a whole company of naked plaster cherubs dancing around the light fixture on the ceiling.

And instead of gray steel lockers, coat hooks in the wood paneling of the corridors. She leaned against the wall and settled her head between Alyssa and Barbara. Alyssa with the curly black hair and Barbara with the single braid. Alyssa, who would show her to her desk and be her partner in line, and Barbara, who would carry her notebook. Alyssa, who would gather all the other girls close to her over the scattering of jacks on the pavement and pass secret notes across her desk to Barbara, who would whisper her name in the corridor and imitate her walk. Alyssa, who with the point of her black pen would draw a large X across the back of Maggie's blouse, and Barbara, who would squeeze out a scribble of glue across the seat of her desk.

Maggie turned now to the smooth green sleeve of Alyssa's lovely jacket and, grasping it tightly in both hands, contorted it into a violent, burning twist. Tighter and tighter she twisted it until, when it would turn no more, she let it snap back like a sprung coil. Next she moved to Barbara's sleeve, twisting it sharply to the back of the neckhole and pressing its cuff against the collar until she could almost hear a squeal of pain issue from the missing head. Down the row she went, twisting one sleeve after another into vicious knots until they all swung limply like the broken swing on its single rope.

Any minute now the classroom door would open and the teacher would step out into the corridor. "Your new classmates are all looking forward to meeting you, Maggie," she would say, smiling.

But Maggie would no longer be there.

The long corridors were confusing, and some of the stairways led only to dead ends. In time Maggie found herself standing on a fire escape two, no, three floors above the ground. She clutched the railing and looked down at the playground below. Everything lay in a geometric design: a circle of dodge-ball players, a square of box ball, a triangle of girls huddled over a throw of jacks, a set of parallel lines on either side of a volleyball net, a baseball diamond. Only she, Maggie, high above on the fire escape, was part of no shape, and she remained alone, a single point, with her hands wrapped on the iron rail.

The air was cold and the wind whipped her thighs, making them quiver. "What's that?" the Backwoods Girls asked, for she had called them to her and they all crowded along the railing.

"That's my playground. I'm letting those children play in it while I'm not using it."

"Ooh. What's a playground?"

"It's a place where you play games."

"Ooh, how wonderful. Can we play?"

"Maybe later, when everybody's gone. Not now."

"Tell us what they're playing."

"Over there, in the circle, they're—"

"Look!" a voice cried out from below, and suddenly the playground was frozen still. "It's the new girl! Up on the fire escape!" In the next moment, the geometric designs had broken into a hundred splinters, and Maggie could hear footsteps on the stairs inside. "How come you ran away?" They were crowding at the door that led to the fire escape. "You're not allowed out here." "They've been looking all over for you." "You're supposed to go to the principal's office; she said to send you there." "What are you staring at?" "What are you looking at me like that for?" "You better come in. You're not supposed to be here." "Stop looking like that." "How come she's staring like that?" "Why doesn't she say something?" "Maybe she doesn't speak English." "Maybe she doesn't speak at all." "Maybe she's crazy." "Hey, she's wearing my hat. Hey, give me my hat back!" "Hey, she spat at me." "Hey, *stop* that!"

Maggie waited on the fire escape until they had all gone. She leaned once more over the railing, watching them come out in ones or twos to take up their positions again on the playground, and realizing with some satisfaction that for the first time ever she had managed to skip entirely the brief period when everyone would try to be nice.

CHAPTER ELEVEN

❧

At first, in those early weeks, Aunt Harriet and Aunt Lillian continued to bring in friends for Maggie. " 'No man is useless while he has a friend,' " Aunt Lillian announced, quoting from something. The granddaughter of a woman Aunt Harriet knew from some health society came once, and so did the daughter of the man who mowed the lawn. A boy came— Maggie wasn't sure who he was; he sat at the parlor window setting the drapery fringes into a tangle of knots and he left, without having said a word, an hour later when Aunt Lillian came to tell him his visit was over. But no one ever came back and no one ever invited Maggie anywhere; in time the aunts gave up on their invitations and no one came at all.

Each afternoon Maggie walked home from school alone,

hurrying past pairs of girls—all those pairs of girls with canvas bags slung over their shoulders and handfuls of peanuts cupped at their mouths. Sometimes someone would call after her, "Saggy, baggy, faggy Maggie," and the name would hit the back of her head in four solid punches, but she would walk fast, keeping her eyes fastened on the outline of the gray stone building rising above the trees—her home now.

Her only visitors were the Backwoods Girls, and they came every day. "Ooh, what's this?" they asked, as Maggie showed them around the kitchen. "That's a stove," she explained. "Watch what happens when I turn this handle." "Ooh, how scary," they cried as a circle of blue flame sprang up without warning.

No one came even to visit her aunts. Uncle Morris didn't come. Maggie hadn't seen him since that first day when he stood in the garden doorway and admired her in her aunts' curlers and silver slippers streaked with grass juice. "Enchanting," he had exclaimed, and then again, "Enchanting," as Maggie struggled up the stairway with her aunts. "Morris, be still," one of them had called down to him as Maggie tried to yank her elbow away from her aunts' grip. "Morris," the other one snapped, "I think it's time you took your leave."

"Ah, my leave," he had called back. And then, "Has anyone seen my leave?" By now they were at the top of the stairs and Maggie was trying to kick first one aunt and then the other. "Maggie, have you seen my leave?" More struggling, and then, from farther away: "What a shame to lose one's leave." A pause. "Leaves don't grow on trees, you know."

"Morris!" both aunts had called down together as they steered Maggie across the upstairs hall. Then, "I will be back," he had said. "I will be back before the first snowflake," and those were the last words of his she had heard.

There had been some snowflakes, early ones, and Maggie had wondered about him that day as she gazed through the frozen tracings on her classroom window and later on when she hurried beside the whitened blades of grass on her way home. Would his silver-headed walking stick and black bowler be hanging on the clothes rack when she opened the door? But he hadn't come, and her aunts' hats—one black, one green—swung alone on the dragon arms in the front hall.

The house was always silent now. The two aunts moved about as though on tiny rubber wheels, gliding from room to room, polishing a tabletop, lifting a vase, replacing it. Each afternoon Aunt Harriet would sit at the rolltop desk in the parlor and write letters. Maggie sometimes looked over the envelopes laid out on the hall table and wondered what the letters said. Did any of them mention her? Among all those letters, did the name Maggie ever appear? Maggie goes to the New Academy, maybe? Maggie made her bed today? Maggie is *here*, even?

When her aunts spoke at all it was to deliver a lecture.

"Eight to ten glasses of water a day," Aunt Lillian said, before Maggie left for school in the morning. "Water flushes out the system." "Dry your feet," Aunt Harriet said when Maggie returned in the afternoon. "Damp feet lower the body's resistance to germ invasions." "Only a face with character is a face of beauty," Aunt Lillian said, catching her as she stared at herself in the hall mirror, and Maggie wondered if what she said could be true: Only people with "character" were pretty. None of the girls in her class had any character at all, but some of them were amazingly pretty. Randi, who had emptied the salt shaker into Maggie's milk container on her third day of school, had hair that glowed like some kind of orange sun around her face. And Alyssa, who told Maggie every day that her brain was defective, had eyes as blue as dragonfly wings. Maggie tried to imagine what her own face would look like if somehow she had what Aunt Lillian called character. Suppose one day a ray of goodness entered her body. Would it show in her face? Would Aunt Harriet and Aunt Lillian look at her and see beauty where just the day before they had seen cracked lips and straight ropes of sticky hair moistening her cheeks?

"Don't draw phlegm into your throat like that," Aunt Harriet said when Maggie sat at the parlor window. "You will block your ear passages permanently. Think what it would be like never to hear again." She did think of that. What would it be like to be robbed of her hearing by too large a plug of phlegm in her throat? What if she never again heard the words of the girls after school? Never again heard "Saggy, baggy, faggy Maggie"? What if she never again heard the words of her aunts? How long would it take her, in this silent house, to notice that she was deaf?

Part II

PROLOGUE

❦

Last year May fourteenth fell on a Saturday. Today, the Anniversary, was Sunday, and the two little girls who now called Maggie their sister had been playing all afternoon in the backyard. Maggie looked down at them from her room. One of them, the older, was doing what she called "stunts" on the prickly patches of lawn—crooked, incomplete cartwheels that barely cleared the ground—and the other had tipped over the webbed chair to make a tent. In a little while they would tire of their play and would be at Maggie's door. "Tell us some more stories," they would ask. "Tell us about when you put all your clothes in the charity box and about Uncle Morris hiding the cord you turn the light on with."

It was funny telling them about the clothes and the light cord, while all those other things that had happened at Adelphi

Hills remained hidden and untold, a secret forever, as though they had never taken place at all.

Even if she had wanted to tell about them, she wouldn't have known how to begin, or where, because she could never be certain just when the beginning occurred. When did it all start? When exactly? She stared out the window now, hardly seeing her two little sisters anymore, or hearing their calls ("Maggie, look at me! Look at me!"), as she tried once more to remember the first week with her aunts, the second, the third. Which week was it? She screwed up her face, blocking everything from her sight in an effort to call up a memory of the very first sign—the first stirring, the first whisper, the first what?—that led her finally to discover that she and her two aunts did not live in the big gray house alone.

CHAPTER TWELVE

The thing was that it all happened little by little, the way lights go down in an auditorium, so slowly you aren't sure that they're going down at all, but by the time everything is finally dark you feel no surprise.

In the beginning the sounds that penetrated the silence at Adelphi Hills could barely be called sounds at all. Rustles, maybe, or rushings in the air, and so gentle they never caused Maggie's eye to lift from her book, or her hand to waver over the spread of playing cards on her bed. Only later—days? weeks?—could they actually be heard, not just felt, and even then they were small sounds, no louder than the stirring of a clock about to chime or the faraway cry of a flight of geese. Not even whispers. Maggie ignored them as she did the hum of the refrigerator in the kitchen.

Then—she didn't know when—they became tiny murmurs with words she could pick out; little scraps of speech falling here, there, like dried leaves, but far off, as though from a radio left playing in some distant room. "CAREFUL," she heard once, or thought she heard, "IT WILL BREAK," and "GET THE BROOM."

But even then she didn't notice. Not much, anyway. Maybe her aunts had hired someone to work in an unknown region beneath the stairs. Maybe they had put up some visitors in a room she had never seen. Maybe a lot of things. She returned to her cards.

Little by little. So that when one day they spoke so clearly she dropped her fork on the floor, she was startled, yes, but not quite surprised.

"THE ROSES NEED WATERING," someone said, aloud, clearly, from just behind her chair at the dining table, and the fork flew from her hand. "I'LL TAKE THE DOG WITH ME." Maggie's head shot around, but no one was there.

"Who else is in this house?" she demanded, looking from one aunt to the other.

The two old sisters looked up at her in surprise; she rarely spoke at the dinner table.

"Swallow your food before you speak," Aunt Lillian said.

"Who else is here?" Maggie insisted. "Besides us? Who's saying all those things?"

"Who's saying all what things? Chew your food before you swallow it."

"Different things. Like about a dog. And the roses, and a broom sometimes."

Aunt Harriet looked down the table at her sister; two vertical wrinkles appeared above her nose as she drew her brows together. "It's her nerves," she said. "She is high-strung. I knew it the moment I laid eyes upon her. That is a nervous child, I said. Nervous and high-strung. She needs something to calm her down."

"Hot milk at bedtime," Aunt Lillian pronounced, and returned to her dinner.

"It's not my nerves!" Maggie's voice rose. "Somebody is saying things. Somebody said something just now. Somebody's *here*." But her aunts only lifted their heads and gazed down at her. "Don't shout," Aunt Lillian said. "Excitement at mealtimes interferes with digestion. Remember that. Always be calm when you eat."

Maggie stared at them. What was going on here, anyway? Why couldn't her aunts hear voices that were in the same room with them and that spoke as plainly as Maggie did herself? What *were* the voices? Who was there? Or was no one there? Maybe, she thought with a chill, she was going crazy.

Another time: "IT SAYS HERE THERE'S BEEN A FIRE," and Maggie jumped in her chair in the parlor. "Who said that?"

"Lower your voice," Aunt Harriet said from her writing desk, and Aunt Lillian stopped moving the dustcloth up and down the spindles of a chair.

"PRETTY." Or "PITY" maybe. The voice grew faint.

Then louder: "HAVE YOU SET THE TABLE YET?"

"WHICH PLATES SHOULD WE USE?"

"THE ONES WITH THE PANSIES."

"Who's saying all that stuff?" Maggie half rose from her seat.

"Don't say 'stuff,' " Aunt Harriet said briskly, putting down her pen. "It's vulgar."

"Who just said that about a fire and then about plates with pansies or something?"

"Nobody said anything," Aunt Harriet said, and she returned to her letters, moistening their envelopes with a tiny rubber sponge. ("Never lick envelopes or stamps," she had cautioned Maggie once. "They are unclean.")

"You were sleeping in your chair," Aunt Lillian said, going back to her dusting.

"I was not. I was wide awake."

"Sound asleep," Aunt Lillian answered. "I watched you breathe," and then, to Aunt Harriet, "She has poor sleeping habits."

"She gets no exercise," Aunt Harriet said. "No exercise and no fresh air."

"She should take walks," Aunt Lillian said. "From now on there will be a walk every night before bedtime. It's no wonder she falls asleep in her chair."

Still, someone *was* there. She was sure of it. More than some*one*. Some two. Or three—enough for a conversation. Their voices were everywhere now: in the dining room and in the parlor. In the hallway, on the stairs, in her room.

"HOW ABOUT A TURN IN THE GARDEN?" she heard suddenly, as she sat in her window seat, and she jumped up, giving the curtain a violent shake. "NO. I'LL STAY HERE AND REST MY FEET." She cranked the window open as far as it would go, leaning into the blazing light, turning this way, that way, reaching too far out. Who's there? But the garden lay still as a page in a book.

"A TURN IN THE GARDEN WILL CLEAR YOUR HEAD." The voice was in the closet, and Maggie flung open the door. Where are you? The quiet row of dresses hung motionless and unanswering from its pole.

"MY HEAD IS QUITE CLEAR." The wall now, and Maggie

pressed her ear against its surface. Where?

"WE WILL TAKE THE DOG." Another wall, and Maggie rapped it with her knuckles, shriveling her skin.

"BUT HE IS ASLEEP." Still another wall, and Maggie tapped again. Who's there? Who?

Then something about a kettle—a question: something, something "IN THE KETTLE?" from over the sink, and she picked up her toothbrush cup.

In her last school somebody showed her how to listen to conversations in another room by putting a glass to the wall and pressing her ear against its bottom. She tried that now, moving the toothbrush cup about the wall the way a doctor places a stethoscope here and there on a bare chest. But the voices only came and went from one wall to the next, and then traveled out the door—down the hall, in one room and out another. Maggie chased after them, entering rooms that were forbidden to her—Aunt Lillian's, Aunt Harriet's, the children's bedrooms with their empty beds, the old-fashioned schoolroom, the empty room with the varnished floor. But the voices vanished when she approached.

There was a game that the girls in her old school used to play: One girl would search for a hidden thimble and everyone else would cry out "hot" or "cold" as whoever it was—never Maggie—moved uncertainly among the desks and chairs, looking. "Hot, hotter, *burning*," when she drew close. And then, "Warm. Cold. *Freezing*," as, maddeningly, she moved farther and farther away from the silver thimble tucked neatly into the water faucet at the sink. Maggie thought of that now as she put one foot in front of the other and waited, listening for some clue that would tell her where to look. Where *were* they? Where were they hiding? Was she hot or cold?

She heard them in the garden.

"BACK SO SOON?" She was sitting in the little rooms laid out with sticks under the birches. "IT WAS TOO COOL," and she moved her ear about the tree trunk like a divining rod in search of treasure.

What *were* they? Voices without people? Why could only she hear them? If she was imagining them, why did she hear them only in and around the house, never in school? Suddenly she remembered what Jeanette had said during her visit about how the house was haunted, and she remembered something else: a fleeting face in some high window, caught by her eye like a sunbeam, as she moved from the car up the front walk the day she arrived.

CHAPTER THIRTEEN

"WHERE IS THE PARASOL?" Maggie heard early one morning when her head was still heavy and only a deep-gray light edged her window curtain. The voice was loud and clear, and Maggie sat up in bed, listening. "THE GREEN SILK PARASOL. FOR THE GARDEN. I NEVER REMEMBER WHERE I'VE PUT IT. HELP ME. HELP ME FIND IT," the voice commanded, commanded *her*, Maggie thought, and she slipped out of bed and opened the door, listening into the dark hallway. "HELP ME LOOK!"

"Okay," Maggie said, and she advanced down the hall. "IT CAN'T BE THERE. I NEVER LEAVE IT THERE."

"Then where?" Maggie cried out. "Where should I look?"

and her words rang, shrill and trembling, along the hall. "Where?"

A bedroom door opened.

"What's going on here?"

Maggie jumped, startled, and faced Aunt Harriet standing in her doorway. "What are you doing here, waking everybody up?" Aunt Harriet spoke in an angry whisper, and her hair, rolled into pink plastic sausages, bounced with every word.

In another moment a second door opened, and Aunt Lillian was in the hallway, shivering slightly in her nightgown, her hair hanging like trailing weeds around her shoulders. "Who's shouting? What is all of this? What are you doing here, Maggie?"

"I'm looking for something."

"What are you looking for at five o'clock in the morning?"

"A para— Nothing. My handkerchief. I lost it."

"Get back to your room. You don't have a handkerchief," and the two bedroom doors closed with little quiet clicks.

"HERE IT IS," she heard as she returned to her room.

"AH, OF COURSE. UNDER THE CHAIR WHERE I LEFT IT."

They hadn't been commanding her at all, whoever they were. They didn't even know she was there. They spoke only to each other, and she just listened in, as though some crossed wires exposed a distant telephone conversation to her ear.

By then the voices spoke every day, and Maggie drifted slowly into their world. She had given up trying to locate them, or even to find an explanation for them. They had become, somehow, a part of the house, like the gray feathered wallpaper in the parlor, except that they belonged only to her, and she listened to them as she listened to voices in a dream. She had learned finally to distinguish between them— there were, in fact, only two: a man's and a woman's.

"THE KETTLE NEEDS SCOURING." The woman's voice was speaking, and Maggie stopped on the stairway, imagining a tarnished kettle with a battered spout hissing on a stove in some far-off room she had never seen.

"DID YOU REMEMBER TO WATER THE ROSES?" The man's voice this time, and Maggie pictured a bed of roses abloom in some other garden. Water them, she urged no one, some-one. Water them before they all die.

"THE DOG WILL WANT TO GO OUT," she heard, and she created a picture in her head of an impatient dog, brown maybe, with a white tail, scratching at some faraway door. Let him out, she thought. Open the door.

Where was it? Where was the door? Where were the kettle and the rose garden? Where was the dog? Where were the people who spoke?

"HOW SOON BEFORE WE SHOULD CALL HER?" Maggie was in the upstairs hall. Call who, she wondered. Me?

"WE WANT TO MAKE SURE SHE IS THE RIGHT ONE. WHAT IF WE MAKE A MISTAKE?"

The right one. Somebody had said that to her once. "You're the right one," something like that. She couldn't remember who.

"WE WON'T MAKE A MISTAKE. LET'S CALL HER SOON."

"Call who?" Maggie said aloud.

"WE WILL CALL HER AS SOON AS WE ARE CERTAIN."

"Call who?" Maggie repeated into the hall.

"THERE'S STILL A LOT TO DO."

"EVERYTHING TAKES SO LONG."

"Answer me!" Another voice, different this time. "Answer when I call you. Stop staring like that. *Answer* me."

"Call who?" Maggie asked again.

And then, from behind the wall: "UNDO THESE BUTTONS."

"Look at me." The other voice again. "I've been calling you for five minutes!"

"Call who?" Maggie asked, louder still. "Me?"

She felt the sharp sting across her cheek before she realized what it was. Aunt Harriet was standing in front of her, her face angry and red, her hand hanging limply in the air. "Stop being rude," she shouted. Maggie hadn't heard her shout before, and her voice sounded funny. "Why did you make me come all the way upstairs to find you?" She was out of breath, and her words came in little spurts. "Why didn't you answer when I called?"

"I didn't hear you," Maggie answered. "I mean, I thought it was somebody else."

"I will not tolerate rudeness," Aunt Harriet went on. "Go to your room. And make your bed. You've forgotten again. And stop sucking your hair."

Maggie rubbed her cheek. Neither aunt had ever slapped her before, and the idea of it, along with the force of the blow, made her dizzy. She rested her head against the wall. The voices—the other ones—had stopped now, and all she could hear was her aunt moving quickly, more quickly than usual, down the stairs.

Call who? she wondered again as she drifted back to her room. Me?

"Look," she said to the Backwoods Girls. "See this? This is a window. Watch what happens when I turn this handle."

"Ooh, how wonderful," they answered, as the window slowly swung open. "Let me try. Let *me*, let *me*, let *me*."

"No," Maggie answered. "You'd only break it," and she stretched her body far out into the open air. Beneath her the lawn rippled like a snakeskin in the sun. The chrysanthemums blazed yellow and gold in their beds, and a spear of light bouncing off the blade of a hoe stung her eyes. To her right the remaining pale leaves on the birch trees quivered like shells on a wind chime. "Ooh, how far you're leaning out!" the five girls cried. "You'll fall." "No, I won't. But don't you try it," Maggie cautioned, and she reached out farther still. "Ooh, how high we all are," the girls exclaimed, crowding around her.

Suddenly Maggie saw something move among the shadows of the birches, and she twisted her body around to get a better look. Someone was sitting against the trunk of one of the trees; a pair of legs moved, and now an arm. The Backwoods Girls fell back as Maggie gazed into the afternoon light. Who was it? Who was invading her trees, shattering her shadows, sitting in her little kitchen all laid out with sticks? All at once something silver flashed—the knob of a walking stick. It was Uncle Morris's, and a moment later she saw the half-moon of his black hat against the white bark.

There had been a time when she almost wanted Uncle Morris to visit again, but now, at the sight of his hat against the birches—her birches—she grew impatient and angry. "Go away," she cried out. "Those are *my* trees," but he didn't hear; his legs remained stretched out on the lawn, and the bowler was a stationary blot on the bark. "Go away," she snapped instead at the Backwoods Girls, and in an instant she was alone in her silent room. She crossed to the mirror and stared at the three pink streaks staining her cheek—Aunt Harriet's slap. Call who? she wondered again. The voices were quiet now, and she returned to the window seat. Her eye wandered back and forth across the garden, coming to rest finally on the birch trees and on Uncle Morris, who still sat beneath them. She looked at him for a long time before it finally—and suddenly—came to her that it was he who had once said something about being the right one. "I think you are the right one after all," he had said. It was on the day she arrived, in the dining room.

Right one for what?

CHAPTER FOURTEEN

⋰⋱

It was a hot afternoon, ridiculously hot for early November, hot even in the shade of the birches. Little pools of sweat had begun to collect in the hollows behind Maggie's knees, and the grass had left a tangled imprint on the heel of her hand. Now and then a bee, tricked into thinking it was summer, came to rest on the open blossom of a late-blooming rose and rubbed its feet across the soft yellow dust inside. Idly, Maggie watched a leaf from a branch overhead float on the still air and land on a pleat of her skirt. A silent afternoon. The voices had not spoken since early that morning when she heard what sounded like a squabble behind the staircase wall:

"I'M GROWING IMPATIENT! HOW MUCH LONGER MUST WE WAIT?"

"IT ISN'T TIME YET. WE CAN'T BE SURE. WHAT IF SHE ISN'T RIGHT?"

"NONSENSE."

"WAIT A LITTLE LONGER. UNTIL WE'RE SURE."

"I'M GETTING TIRED OF IT."

Now she sat among the little rooms on the grass, and moved one stick back and forth like a door, so she could walk her fingers from one room to the next and back again: kitchen to dining room to kitchen. In and out. A crow fluttered in the sky like a black handkerchief and folded itself neatly on the edge of a chimney. Suddenly something moved among the shadows of the distant trees, and once again Maggie saw the flash of a silver knob and a bowler hat outlined like a little black hill against the sky.

Uncle Morris had been back several times since she had seen him from her window, the day her face had been slapped by Aunt Harriet. His visits always came as a surprise. Her aunts never told her he was coming, never said, "Go wash your face, your uncle Morris will be here today." He would just *be* there. She would look up from her book or away from the window in the parlor, and there he would be, standing on the rug and saying something for which she could find no answer.

"Aha!" he said once, making her jump in her chair, where she had been staring at the pictures over the mantel, sucking her hair, doing nothing. "For a moment," he said, "I thought you were someone else. There used to be someone here by the name of Maggie. Would you know her? She looked a little like you, but her eyes were brown and yours," he said, leaning close to her face, "are purple."

Nobody had ever teased her like that before—to be funny, not mean—and for a moment she tried to think up something funny to say back. Something that would make him laugh, maybe, or say, "Maggie, that was a wonderful thing you just said." Sometimes, alone in her room, she made Uncle Morris say nice things about her in her head. "She is a clever child," he would remark to someone. "Clever beyond her years." Or, to her, "That was a quite good joke," and he would smile a small smile. But now she could think of nothing funny to say at all.

"They're brown," she finally managed.

"Purple," he insisted, peering into her face again. "Purple as a bunch of grapes. Purple as daffodils."

Maybe, instead of answering with a joke, she could go on saying dumb things until after a while he would feel sorry for teasing her so long and he would say something nice. "But I'm only *teasing*." Something like that. Maybe he would rumple her hair.

"Daffodils aren't purple," she said.

"*Purple* daffodils are. Here, let me show you in the mirror."
He pulled her from her chair and conducted her to the clothes
rack in the front hall. "Look," he said, but suddenly she
was struck with the idea that maybe he wasn't joking at all.
"Look at your purple eyes," he said, but she kept her lids
tightly closed, not wanting to look, afraid that in the next
moment she would find two grape-colored eyes staring at
her from a face that wasn't her own.

"They're brown," she said, looking at herself at last.

"Hmm," Uncle Morris said, and then again, "Hmm. Something must be wrong with the mirror," and he struck its
frame a swift blow. "Lillian!" he called down the hall. "Have
you had this mirror checked lately? It needs oil or something.
It's misbehaving again. It makes this child's eyes look brown,
when they're really purple. It makes her look like that other
girl who used to be here—Maggie, whatever her name was.
Maybe it needs new batteries. Lillian?"

"They're brown," Maggie repeated, feeling stupid, but still
she wondered. What if her eyes were purple and she didn't
know it? What if she were somebody else and not the person
she had been yesterday?

"Morris is a fool," Aunt Harriet would say after each of
his visits. "He has the mind of a silly boy."

Funny to think of Uncle Morris as a boy, silly or not, Maggie
thought now as she watched him approach her across the
lawn on this hot afternoon. Uncle Morris a boy? Tall Uncle

[117]

Morris? So tall he could blow tiny dust storms across the books on the top shelf of the parlor bookcase or put the end of the light cord on the door lintel where no one could reach it or, in the dark, find it?

"I can't find the light cord!" Aunt Lillian cried out in alarm one night. They had all come into the front hall after one of those nighttime walks that were supposed to make Maggie sleep better. "Harriet, the light cord is gone," and the two aunts began sweeping their arms about in the dark as though they were casting a spell or striking at cobwebs in front of their faces. "It's been cut!" Aunt Harriet exclaimed, and Maggie caught her breath. Finally Aunt Lillian groped her way down the hall and returned with a flashlight. "There it is," she said. "On the lintel. How did it get up *there?*" "Morris's doing, most likely," Aunt Harriet said as she ran a yardstick along the door ledge and the smooth oval knob finally swung wildly down on its cord, hitting their outstretched hands. "It is one of his jokes."

"Morris's jokes are not amusing," Aunt Lillian said, blinking in the sudden light.

It was true, Maggie thought now as he drew closer and rubbed the edge of his hat on his sleeve. His jokes never made anyone laugh—they weren't even jokes. really—but he continued to play them anyway. The same ones. During each of his next visits he silently put the light cord up on the door ledge, when no one was amused or, after a while, even fooled by it. The last time, Maggie swept it down herself with the yardstick, right after he left, before her aunts could discover it themselves late at night. "No sense at all," Aunt Lillian said, and yet, somehow, it *was* funny, sort of, and Maggie laughed a little now and then, not aloud, but quietly, behind her ribs.

Uncle Morris stood at her feet now. What would he tell her this time? That her hair was blue? That she was a gnome? That she wasn't there, even—she had become invisible? She waited. "I've brought a book," he announced, and he stepped respectfully around the little lines of sticks on the ground. "*Puck of Pook's Hill*," he read from the cover. "The title is nice to say—say it, Maggie: *Puck of Pook's Hill*—but the story makes little sense. It's about fairies," and he lowered himself carefully next to her, settling himself within the outlines of the little dining room. "Fairies," he went on, gazing at her solemnly, "are the creatures who buy up all those used teeth."

The tooth fairy. Sometimes girls in her old schools would tell of putting a tooth under the pillow at night and finding a dime or a quarter in its place the following morning, and once, long ago, Maggie herself had tried it, but she had found nothing the next day except the tooth itself, its edges traced with the dried blood from her raw gum. He waited for her to answer.

"There's no such thing," she said.

"No such thing!" Uncle Morris looked offended. "No such

thing? Maggie, do you know that some fairies have been known to spend as much as an entire *dollar* on a single molar? And you say there's no such thing? A dollar for one tooth! And do you know why?"

She put a strand of hair in her mouth.

"They make *drinks* out of them!" Uncle Morris explained. "Drinks! Did you know that? They drop each tooth into a buttercup of boiling dew, and let it steep for a few minutes, and then they drink the liquor."

Maggie scraped off a thin channel of pale-green scum from the rock under her knee and rubbed it along her thumbnail.

"Save that," Uncle Morris said, observing her. "That's frog makeup. They use it around their eyes."

Maggie examined her tinted nail and wondered for a moment what it would be like to brighten the eyelid of a frog with its yellow-green film. Just a slender circle, she thought, one here, one here.

"Here," Uncle Morris offered. "We'll collect it on this leaf," and for a brief moment Maggie held out her thumb, but she withdrew it quickly and wiped it clean on the edge of the rock.

"And do you know what they call it," he went on, "this wonderful liquor brewed from the molars of thousands of young mouths across the land?" He looked at her. "Do you know?"

"No."

Uncle Morris lowered his head and his voice at the same time. "Tooth tea," he said confidentially. "Tooth tea. But sometimes their tongues get tangled, and they call it 'two teeth' instead, which confuses the fairy cooks no end—they put two molars into a single buttercup instead of one, and that makes the tea too tart. Then the fairies become angry, and they all start yelling at once, 'The two-teeth tooth tea is too, too tart.' Sometimes you can hear them, late at night, although most people mistake the sound for the chirping of crickets. Have you ever heard them?"

Maggie said the words to herself, catching her tongue on the backs of her teeth. The two-teeth tooth tea is too, too tart. It *did* sound like the chirp of a cricket, a little. How did he think those things up?

"Have you heard them?" Uncle Morris repeated.

"No."

He lifted the book and turned the pages slowly on his knee. "The book begins," he said, "with a song. Except it isn't a song at all, because there's no music to it, which makes it a poem, and a boring one at that, so we'll skip over it." That was nice to hear. Maggie always skipped over the poems in books, even if they were only two lines long.

Then Uncle Morris began to read aloud. He read as she had never heard anyone read before, as though he were actually *speaking* to her, telling a story in words that came to him at the moment, and Maggie leaned over now and then to see if the phrases he spoke were the same as those on the page. For a long while she tried to follow the tale, watching his face as he read, but the book was old and the sentences complicated, and she eventually gave up listening. She watched, instead, the crow, rising now from the chimney and spilling its cry into the sky. In time Uncle Morris's voice began to falter, and he marked the place in his book with a blade of grass. His eyelids closed and his mouth opened. He had fallen asleep, and Maggie found herself counting the beat of his breathing: in-two-three-four, out-two-three-four. In. Out. In. Out.

Then, from the trees behind her, the voices spoke.

"PERHAPS WE SHOULD GET A NEW WASHTUB."

"BUT I HAVE A WASHTUB."

"MAYBE YOU COULD HAVE ANOTHER. IT SAYS HERE THERE ARE WASHTUBS FOR SALE."

"WHAT WOULD I DO WITH ANOTHER WASHTUB?"

"ONE COULD BE FOR THE CLOTHES AND ONE COULD BE FOR THE DOG. FOR HIS BATH."

"BUT HE NEVER NEEDS A BATH."

Uncle Morris stirred in his sleep just then. "He might like one just the same," he said aloud.

"Mmm," Maggie agreed. The dog, wherever he was, might like a bath. And then she sat straight up and stared at her uncle. What? What did he say? "What did you say?" she demanded. "What did you just say?" Had he heard the voices, too? Uncle Morris?

He shifted his arm. "He might like one just the same," he repeated, his eyes still closed.

"He might like *what*?" Maggie was shaking his arm now. "Like *what* just the same? A bath? *Who* might like one just the same? The dog?"

Uncle Morris opened his eyes slowly. "What's that?" he asked.

"You said, 'He might like one just the same.' "

"Sounds as though I was having a wicked dream."

"But *they* had said, 'The dog never needs a bath.' "

"Who said the dog never needs a bath? Dogs always need a bath. The first thing I say when I meet a dog is, 'You need a bath.' "

"*They* said that. Those people. Whoever they are. The ones who talk in the walls and in these trees. They said that about the dog, and then you said—"

"Maggie, you're going too fast for me."

"Who are they?" Maggie had her face next to his by now, and a little spray of her spit touched his cheek as she spoke. "You heard them—those voices. Who are they? Who *are* they? Who? Who else is here?" She was shaking both his shoulders now. *"Who?"*

"Maggie, I can't follow a word you're saying."

"But you heard them. You *did*. You answered them. They said . . . " Her voice broke.

Uncle Morris bent over her. "Is that a tear?" he asked, and with the point of his finger he lifted the drop that had fallen on Maggie's cheek. "I do believe it is. Maggie, somebody dropped a tear on your face and then ran away. Do you think whoever it is wants it back? Shall we try to find him? Or her? It looks like a very special tear. If it were mine, I wouldn't have been so careless with it. It can certainly be used many times again, by the looks of it. Come, let's try to find its owner, and if we can't we'll just keep it for ourselves in a little jar. It's always nice to have a spare tear around. You never know when you might need one." He lengthened himself out in sudden snapping movements, like a carpenter's folding rule, and pulled himself up from the ground. "Let's have a look." He held out his finger, with her tear still glistening at its end, and walked in long strides toward the house.

Maggie rose to follow him. "Who are they?" she persisted when she had caught up. "Where do they come from? Who's saying all those things? Where are those people? What are those voices?"

"The voices?" Uncle Morris turned to look down at her, and for a long time he said nothing at all. He just *looked* with the same expression he had worn on her first day here when her aunts tore the pink curlers from her head and unclasped the chain at her throat. "Enchanting," he had said then, as though he really liked looking at her.

"Ah, the voices," he said now, and Maggie's heart jumped. "There are, as it happens, many voices," and he looked off into the distance. "The one I like best belongs to the pigeon. Low and murmury. But the frog, too, has a nice voice. When he speaks, that is. His singing voice is terrible." The little teardrop still clung like a glass ladybug to the ball of his finger. She watched it catch the light and, for a brief instant, sparkle. "And that is all I can contribute today to the subject of voices," Uncle Morris concluded. He looked down at her with what might have been a smile. She put her hair in her mouth and said nothing, standing still in the center of the lawn and not following when he finally turned and strode toward the house, carrying her tear away on his finger.

He heard them, she said to herself. He heard the voices.

CHAPTER FIFTEEN

❧⬥❧

"Stand up straight!" Maggie commanded, and the five Backwoods Girls stood at immediate attention. "Now take your places," and one after another the barefoot girls marched across the old schoolroom at the end of the upstairs hall and sat down among the rows of connected desks with the empty inkwells and fancy iron legs.

Maggie stood at the front of the room, facing them. "You, Kate," she ordered, pointing to the first seat. "Go to the globe and locate Africa."

"Ooh," answered Kate. "What's a globe?"

"Don't you even know what a globe is? It's this thing. See? This is the globe. It's like the world." Maggie laid her hand on the smooth brown-and-yellow sphere all decorated with sailing ships and mermaids holding shells to their ears like telephone receivers. "Now find Africa on it."

"Africa? What's Africa?"

"Africa's a continent, dummy. Don't you even know that?" She gave the globe a spin that blended the continents, the sea, and all its mermaids and ships into a smear of tan. "Here," she said, stopping it with her finger. "Here's Africa. No, here, I mean."

"Ooh, how wonderful! Africa!"

"Sit down. Elizabeth!" Maggie ordered next. "Your turn. Stand up when you speak," and she waited long enough for the next Backwoods Girl to get to her feet. "Go to the blackboard."

"Ooh, what's a blackboard?"

"What's a blackboard," Maggie repeated in disdain. "This is a blackboard, stupid. Don't you know that? You write on it with chalk"—except there was no chalk, and Maggie wet her finger to write her name. "See?" she said, watching the letters fade and leave a pale imprint. "Now, what's eight times seven? Write the answer on the blackboard."

"Eight times seven? What's that?"

"It's multiplication, that's what. Eight times seven is fifty-six. Say that."

"Fifty-six."

"No, say, 'Eight times seven is fifty-six.' Never mind. You're too dumb. Sit down. Now we'll have reading," and she took five books from the shelf under the window. "Here," she said, placing them, all with frayed bindings and faded lettering, on five empty desks. "Anne, you may begin." She picked up one of the books. "Stand up and read aloud. I'll help you with the words you don't know." But when she opened the book she discovered there were no printed words. Instead, the pages were handwritten, in ink the color of mosquitoes—not brown, not gray; no color, really—and in a hand shaped like mosquitoes, too: tiny winged letters marching across the page on slender legs. "February 17," she read. "More snow today." It was somebody's diary. "Margaretta hid too long in the garden," it went on, "and when she came in at last her nose was blue-gray and her little wrists were flaming. We thawed her out by the stove, although that is not wise. Rub snow on her is what we should have done, but that is cruel, it seems to me, and so she sat by the fire, looking like a roasting goose, with steam rising from her feet and her face growing redder and redder."

Maggie turned the book over in her hand and squinted at the rubbed-out letters on its cover. *Daily* something, it said, and then there were some numbers. One-something. One-eight. Eighteen. Eighteen-something. A date. She ran her fingers over the lettering and a scattering of gold flecks clung to her skin, but she could read nothing further. Somebody's diary, she thought, and she flipped through its pages. Fewer than half were filled, and they stopped abruptly in

May. Probably got kicked out of school, she thought, like me, and she studied the tiny writing some more. Some of the paper was stained with water and looked like watercolors of brown lakes against a sky of cream. "March 18," she read on another page. "A strange day. Louisa and Emily put on their play, but . . ."

"What is going on here?"

Maggie spun around and faced Aunt Lillian and Aunt Harriet in the doorway. "What are you doing in this room?" Aunt Lillian demanded. "Who gave you permission to come in here?"

"Put those books down!" Aunt Harriet's voice rose to a high pitch and abruptly fell. "Look what she's done with the books," she added in a hoarse whisper.

"Come over here," Aunt Lillian ordered. "Come here at once," but Maggie stood where she was, the old diary still in her hand. She stared hard at her two aunts, waiting for them to lower their eyes and move away, but this time they stared back. "Take her to her room," Aunt Lillian finally said, and in the next moment the diary was pulled from her grasp and a hand on her shoulder steered her away from the desks and the blackboard and the globe and the books and the five Backwoods Girls with their bare feet and wondering stares.

The next time Maggie tried the schoolroom door, it was locked.

CHAPTER SIXTEEN

◦◦◦

The day before Thanksgiving was Founders Day at New Adelphi Hills Academy, and, surprisingly, it was to be celebrated at Aunt Lillian's and Aunt Harriet's house, in the parlor. Each year, Maggie learned, all the children from the New Academy trooped down the road to sit in front of the portraits of the two founders of the original school and to listen to speeches about them. And because it was almost Thanksgiving, that holiday was celebrated on the same day, although at one time there had been separate celebrations on separate days. Now the traditions were all mixed together; along with the speeches about the founders, there was a ceremony with candles and a class wish, and everybody brought a bundle of old clothes to contribute to poor people.

The two aunts prepared for the occasion by arranging branches of colored leaves on the mantel and lining up a row of plastic bins in the hallway. The bins were for the old-clothes collection. Later in the afternoon a truck would come and carry them all away, "for the unfortunate," Aunt Harriet had said. "There are children not far from here who would be happy to own a good warm coat and a pair of sturdy shoes." Maggie wondered if that was true. Could there be, down the road, maybe, or over the hill, a family of *real* Backwoods Girls who would *really* marvel over her toothbrush and her ball-point pen?

Now everybody wound along the long road from the school building to the big stone house.

Maggie had seen a picture once of children being evacuated from some European city during World War II—an endless line of boys and girls with oversized ears and black smudges for eyes, all trudging along a bleak highway with bundles of clothes clasped to their chests. She thought of them now as she took her place in line with all the children of her school, each carrying a brown paper bag fat as a pig, and marching with it to the big gray house that could have been a stone fortress.

They had been told not to talk along the way, but only Maggie was silent.

"Hey, Diana, what did you bring?"

"Oh, a bunch of stuff. My sister's old shoes and this old

jacket I haven't worn in a billion years and my last year's denim vest."

"Your denim vest? The one with the parrot on the back? With the sequins? You're giving that away?"

"Yeah, well, it's too small, and anyway I cut the parrot off first and saved it, except the sequins all fell off. What are you bringing?"

"I don't know. Some old stuff. My mother packed it for me. Gloves, mostly, and my sneakers that the toes came through."

"Hey, Gregory, quit stepping on the back of my shoes."

"Well, why can't you walk faster?"

"Hey, look at Maggie's bundle."

"How come she's got such a big bag?"

"Hey, Maggie, what do you have in there, an elephant or what?"

"Yeah, what's in there anyway?"

"Where'd she get all that stuff to give away?"

"She probably stole it."

"Hey, let's see what's in there."

"Don't get near her. She kicks."

"Maybe there's a body in there."

"Yeah, I bet she kicked somebody to death and stuffed the body in that paper bag."

"Two bodies, I bet. It's big enough."

"Hey, Edwin, what did you bring?"

"Me? Oh, my mother's sweater that she doesn't wear any-more and this hat that my grandmother gave me last year that I hate. You should see it. It's got this dumb face like a clown's on it, and the *face* is wearing a hat. So it's like two hats. It's really dumb."

"I brought something that isn't clothes. It's a tablecloth, but my mother said somebody could use it."

"For what? To wear, you mean?"

"No, dummy. For a tablecloth."

"But the teacher said it has to be clothes."

"Well, maybe somebody could wear it. Like for a shawl or something."

"What's the matter with it? I mean, how come you're giving it away?"

"It's got this wine spilled on it that didn't come out."

Along the road they marched, across the front walk, up the wide stone steps, and into the front hall. One by one they paused at the big plastic bins and dropped their bundles in. When it was Maggie's turn she pushed down all the paper bags before laying down her own fat bundle with its rolls of brown dresses, taken that morning from her closet, the long brown stockings from her dresser drawer, the long pink underpants, the undershirts, the slips, and, in the very center, the rubber-faced doll with its pink dress and lace-trimmed underwear.

She felt strange entering her own parlor as though she were a visitor, and when she sat on the floor she looked around at the tables and chairs pushed against the wall and at the china ballerina in the cabinet, as though for the first time. Some things *were* new to her: the branches of autumn leaves, looking strangely bright against the gloom of the parlor wall, and a heavy, eight-stick candlestand that had been placed in front of the fireplace. Strangest of all, though, was the sight of all these children arranged in rows—little ones close to the fireplace, older ones near the windows—on the flowers and vines of the rug of the gray, quiet parlor.

Suddenly Aunt Lillian was speaking. She was wearing a dress Maggie had never seen before, and a circle of pink had been rubbed over the freckles on each cheek. Aunt Harriet, standing at the parlor entrance and greeting everyone, had also rouged her face, except her spots were more purple than pink and contained little dark rivers where the wrinkles were.

"On this day," Aunt Lillian was saying, "we all remember the two personages"—and here she waved her hand to the pale faces on the wall—"who, out of a spirit of charity and love of learning, established Adelphi Hills Academy over one hundred years ago for the purpose of improving the character and stimulating the intellect of a group of carefully chosen girls. . . ."

Maggie stopped listening.

One of the teachers stood up next and asked, "Who has something to share with us about our founders?"

No one answered.

"What do we like to remember about the founders of Adelphi Hills Academy?" the teacher persisted, while Aunt Lillian looked over the rows of faces. Maggie dropped her eyes to the rug and scratched an M into its nap. Aunt Lillian didn't seem to notice her at all, and Aunt Harriet had said, "Good morning, welcome to Adelphi Hills," to her just as she had to everyone else who entered the parlor.

The children were still wearing their coats, and the room smelled of the school hall.

"Who can tell us something about the founders?"

A hand finally went up. "They were over a hundred years old."

Another hand. "They had a spirit of charity."

"They had a love of learning."

"They had a love of character."

"They chose girls."

"They had a dog," someone said, studying the portrait of the man.

"They had a spirit of charity."

"Spirit of charity has been said," a teacher corrected. "Anything else?"

"They were spooky," somebody said, but in an undertone. Maggie looked up. It was Alyssa, from her class, and she was stretching her mouth into an expression of mock horror as she gazed at the portraits. "Look at them," she whispered to someone next to her, to Barbara. "Look at their spooky eyes." "Yeah," Barbara whispered back. "Two spooks."

"What did the founders do for the Academy?" the teacher asked.

"They spooked it," Alyssa whispered, and she giggled with Barbara.

"They found it," someone said.

"Founded."

"They founded it. Nobody knew it was here until they founded it."

Then it was time for the Thanksgiving wishes. The day before, each class had made up a wish and chosen someone to recite it over a lighted candle in Maggie's parlor. Maggie herself had been chosen to deliver her class's wish, but that had been her teacher's idea. "It's Maggie's house, after all," Miss Hunter had said. The wish was full of words like "peace" and "brotherhood" and "no more pollution," when what everyone really wished for was new clothes and maybe a stereo. Maggie had a wish of her own, but she kept it to herself. "What do you wish for, Maggie?" Miss Hunter had asked. "What would you like to add to the class wish?" and she answered, "Freedom for poor people," but she was thinking instead of how Uncle Morris had heard the voices in the birch trees and would not tell her what he knew about them, would not even acknowledge that he had heard them at all.

"Freedom for poor people, Maggie? Freedom to do what?"

"To be poor," she had answered, and the class laughed, but she barely noticed. She was wondering if Uncle Morris could somehow be made to tell.

Aunt Lillian walked over to the large eight-stick candle stand—one candle for each grade—in front of the fireplace. She held a long, flaming taper and handed it to the children as they came up one by one to recite their class wishes.

"The first grade wishes for happy children all over the world," a boy in a bow tie said, and Aunt Lillian wrapped her hand around his fist while he lit the first candle with the taper.

"The second grade wishes that the whole world will be happy and will have enough food to wear and clothes to eat," a girl said, but nobody noticed until Aunt Lillian corrected her: "Food to *eat* and clothes to *wear*," and then everybody laughed.

Maggie rehearsed her class wish silently while the other candles were being lit. "The sixth grade desires" (Alyssa had suggested "desires" and everybody else voted for it) "an end to tyranny and pollution in all the nations of the world." ("Nations of the world" was Howard's. It got more votes than "throughout the universe," which was Randi's.) "We desire freedom everywhere and new scientific achievements to help mankind and womankind" (Barbara had added "womankind") "in their search for better lives." It was a stupid wish.

The five glowing flames on the candlestand had left an imprint on Maggie's vision—five blue blurs that danced in front of her eyes—and they traveled along with her as she picked her way among the hunched bodies on the floor. She had never spoken in front of a lot of people before, and she was surprised to see the taper tremble and its flame dart nervously when Aunt Lillian placed it in her hand. The wick on the sixth candle sprang to life when she touched it, and she opened her mouth to speak.

"WHERE DID I PUT MY HANDKERCHIEF?" The voice came from somewhere in the fireplace and Maggie turned her head to locate it.

"IT'S IN THE WASH BASKET. ARE YOU SNIFFLY TODAY?"

"NO. I NEED IT TO RUB OUT A SPOT ON THE SUGAR BOWL."

"SOON EVERYTHING WILL BE READY."

"THE TEASPOONS COULD DO WITH A POLISH. THEY'RE LOOKING DULL."

"What is the sixth-grade wish, Maggie?" Miss Hunter was asking. "Speak up."

Maggie bent her ear to the fireplace, but no voice came.

"She forgot," someone said from the floor.

"She would," someone else said.

"Maggie, we are all waiting to hear your wish"—Aunt Lillian this time.

"I wish," Maggie said, still looking intently into the fireplace and holding the flaming taper in front of her. "I wish . . ."

"YES. WE WANT THE TEASPOONS TO GLEAM."

"Who can help Maggie with the sixth-grade wish?" Miss Hunter asked. "Alyssa? Will you recite our class wish for Maggie?"

"I wish," Maggie said, as Alyssa advanced across the rug. "I wish," and she faced the candlestand. "I wish," and her voice was steady and clear. "I wish I could find out who's saying all those crazy things!" But Alyssa was taking the taper from her hand now and beginning, "The sixth grade desires . . ."

CHAPTER SEVENTEEN

It was a Saturday in the middle of December. Each window framed a white landscape. The birches, hung with snow, faded into the white sky, and the white stretch of lawn was smudged only by the occasional inkblot of a crow.

Inside, the house was as quiet as the snow. Aunt Harriet and Aunt Lillian had gone out earlier, their dark figures becoming smaller and smaller on the white driveway, and the house had held a mysterious stillness all morning—holding its breath, almost, as if waiting for something to fall.

Maggie wandered aimlessly up and down the upstairs hall, opening and closing doors as though they were flaps on an Advent calendar. Finally she retreated into her own room and summoned the Backwoods Girls to the window.

"Ooh, what are those?" they cried, crowding around the snow scene. "All those white things flying around?"

"Those are snowflakes, dummies. Haven't you ever seen snow before?"

"Ooh, snow. How wonderful. Open the window so we can see more."

Maggie cranked the window open and stepped aside. "Ooh," they all cried. "Catch them, catch them. Bring them in here. Give me some. Give me, give me, give me."

"You can't catch them," Maggie explained. "Look what happens when you touch them. See? They disappear. I can make them all disappear if I want to, just by touching them. Look, I'm magic. I can make snowflakes die with the tip of my little finger. Watch."

"Ooh, don't kill them. Look, Maggie's killing the snowflakes."

"Dummies. They're just water. Cold, white water in little shapes." She wasn't quite sure herself just what snowflakes were. Crystals, she had learned once, but crystals were those heavy glass ornaments that hung in a fringe of perfect cones around the chandelier, not these wet, shapeless rags that floated against her window, vanishing as they hit. "They're white water," she said.

Little wet specks were blowing against her face, and she closed the window, but she remained on the window seat, gazing out, looking for something new to show the Backwoods Girls, and feeling the inside silence press on her as though it, too, were a blanket of snow.

Suddenly, her room rang with a cry: "MAGGIE!" and again, "MAGGIE! COME!" and her hand flew to her throat. The sound hung in the air, and her room, paralyzed with silence just a moment earlier, became alive. The curtain trembled in some unfelt breeze, and the floorboard sprang beneath her step as she jumped up from the window seat. "MAGGIE! IT'S TIME!" There was a long pause. What was she supposed to do? Answer them? She looked around. Answer who? Where? Finally she stepped forward a little and replied as she did in school when her name was called out in the morning: "Maggie Turner?" "Here," she whispered. "Present." And then, a little louder, "Here," but no one answered, and she put a strand of hair in her mouth, feeling silly talking to the air in her room.

"MAGGIE!" Carefully she opened the door and peered into the hall. The walls were dark and quiet. "COME! WE'RE WAIT-ING! YOU KNOW WHERE." And she did. Suddenly she knew exactly where to go and which door to open, and she sped down the dark hall. "I'm coming!" she shouted as she ran.

The first door, the one that led to the short flight of stairs, was unlatched, but the knob to the schoolroom door turned uselessly in her hands. It was locked, as it had been for weeks.

"Wait!" she shouted, and her voice rushed down the empty hall like a cold wind. In a moment she was in Aunt Harriet's room, sweeping through the jumble of pink curlers in the dresser drawer until she found the ring of keys. "Wait, I'm coming!" and she ran back along the hall with the keys pressing their rows of baby teeth into her palm. "Just a minute," she whispered, as she pushed one key after another into the lock. Her heart raced. Soon the door would open and she would find two strangers waiting for her with their kettle and tea set and dog and broom and everything else that she had somehow come to know over the past weeks. "Here I am," she would say, and they would look at her, pleased. "How nice you are," they would answer, and then maybe they would kiss her.

"Wait. Here it is," she said. A key turned, a hidden spring gave way, the door yielded, and she looked into a room that had no one in it at all. The schoolroom desks were just as she had left them. The globe lay round as a pumpkin in its wooden stand, and the blackboard still bore the imprint of the name she had written with her wet finger. Where were the strangers? Why weren't they here?

"THE TEA WILL COOL!" No, not the schoolroom, after all. The empty room beyond. She crossed to the door in the far wall, and next she was standing in the center of the varnished floor of the room with no furnishings. But no one was here either. Everything was still. Each uncurtained window held a silent storm of snow, but nothing stirred within, and she let out a long sigh. It was all a trick. She looked around and finally walked over to the closet. With a quick jerk she swept the door open, but she knew that it, too, would be empty. Everything was a trick.

"WHAT'S KEEPING HER?" The voice *was* in the closet; she could feel it in the walls, and she stepped back to see over the high shelf. "Who's there?" she whispered, entering again.

"HOW DO I LOOK?"

"LOVELY. JUST RIGHT."

"WE WANT TO LOOK OUR BEST. MAGGIE?"

She ran her hands up and down the closet walls—the wall to the left, the rear wall, the wall hidden in the darkness to the right—when suddenly she came upon something she hadn't seen: a knob. No, not a knob. Knobs were round. This was more like a handle; a latch. The kind that lifted up and down on a screen door.

Very slowly, trying to make no noise at all, she lifted it up and gave a small tug. From somewhere there came the sound of a gentle crack, and she pulled again. This time something—a portion of the wall, it seemed—began to yield, and with the next tug it opened like a door on a hinge. A sudden rush of cold air hit her face, and soon she began to make out the outline of a stairway—dark, worn, and with puffs of dust in the corners of each step. She gazed into its reaches and put out her hand to the wall. It was cold, and her fingers held the smell of its dampness. No sound came. Who's there?

she wanted to ask, but the words lay silent in her throat.

Then: "I AM GROWING RESTLESS."

"MAYBE WE SHOULD WAIT IN THE GARDEN. THE ROSES WILL BE SOOTHING."

"BUT I WANT TO BE HERE WHEN SHE COMES." Maggie's heart pounded, and her ears with it. Very slowly she closed the closet door behind her. She was in darkness now, and she had to feel for the bottom step with her toe.

The stairs were steep and narrow, and she could make out nothing of what lay at their top. With her hands braced against the walls she slowly mounted, two feet to each stair, until a sweep of her foot told her she had reached the last step.

There she stood still, her heel hooked over the edge; a cobweb broke against her arm, and her fingers, meeting a sudden object—a table? a box?—sank into soft dust. At first she could see nothing at all, but then she began to make out the dimensions of an enormous space and the outlines of shapes—massive white shapes, some reaching the ceiling, others stretching along the floor. Giants! she thought, and she backed down a step. Giants in white gowns who had lured her here with the sound of their voices and in the next instant would rise from the floor and . . .

"I THINK SHE'S COMING." The voice came from some distance away; Maggie could see now that the giants were really pieces of furniture—cabinets, maybe, and long tables—

draped in cloth, and she took a step forward.

Far to her left stood another huge piece, but not wrapped in cloth—the back of a wardrobe of some sort—and around its corner was a small window. If Maggie could get over there, she could lift its curtain and let in the light.

"IT WILL BE SOON NOW."

She spread herself against a wall and barely breathed. "Who's there?" she tried to whisper, but again no sound came from her lips.

From the other side of the wardrobe something stirred with the sharp crackle of a newspaper being hurriedly put down. Something—a chair leg, maybe—scraped, the curtain trembled, something else—a dish?—fell and shattered, and a whispered cry of dismay rose: "MERCY!"

Maggie stepped back toward the stairway.

"NOW LOOK. A TEACUP BROKEN. IF SHE DOESN'T HURRY I'LL BREAK SOMETHING MORE. I ALWAYS DROP THINGS WHEN TEA IS LATE." The chair scraped again and something with many parts moved. "MAGGIE!"

She could still escape—edge down the stairs, slip through the closet, and return to the snowflakes at her window. There was still time.

"WHAT'S THE TROUBLE WITH THE BREAD TIN?" The voice was deep now—the man's. "IT DOESN'T OPEN."

"RAP IT ALONG THE EDGE. IT'S STUBBORN. AND WE'LL

NEED ANOTHER TEACUP NOW THAT THIS ONE IS BROKEN. WHAT CAN BE KEEPING HER?"

"WHAT SHALL WE DO WITH THE BROKEN PIECES?"

"LET HER SWEEP THEM INTO THE COAL SCUTTLE."

And then for a long time there was silence. Nothing moved and no voice spoke. Slowly she pushed herself away from the wall, her hands spread out in front of her face as though she were making her way through dense fog. Still no sound came, and she slid one foot in front of the other toward the window on the other side of the wardrobe. She could see a narrow strip of snowflakes edging the curtains like a fringe of dancing pompons, and the wardrobe was close enough for her to touch. She tapped softly against its wall, waiting for someone to call out from the other side, "Come in!" but no one spoke. With just one gesture she could touch the window or peer around the corner, but she stood still, waiting, the silence around her so strong it rang in her ears.

Then she sucked in her breath. Now! she said, and with a sudden plunge she reached out to the curtain and swung it aside, letting in a rush of white light. At the same moment a familiar voice cried out, "AT LAST!" and Maggie stood in what she always called, later on, "the other room."

Part III

PROLOGUE

❦

"Can I try on your dress? The one with the purple flowers all over and the bow in the back that you wore to Aunt Lillian's and Aunt Harriet's party and it puffs out when you turn around?"

The little sisters were in her room now. She had just finished telling them, for the hundredth time probably, about Uncle Morris and the light cord, and about how she had been picked to recite the Thanksgiving wish in the parlor.

"Can I?"

They were like the old Backwoods Girls, always thinking that everything she did was wonderful, and marveling over the few items she had brought with her from Adelphi Hills: the party dress, the rose-bordered handkerchief, the lilac—dried out now and beginning to flake—that she had worn last year in her hair. But the little sisters were real, and Maggie didn't call them dummies or tell them they were too ugly—or too poor—to try on her purple dress. She even did up the buttons for them and tied the belt in the back so the bow lay straight and flat, not up and down.

"Tell us about the party." The little girl's voice came from somewhere inside the dress. She had begun to push herself into it, and the skirt, with its fields of tiny violets, hung from her head like a lampshade. "Tell about the food." The dress suddenly began to dance and shake as she hunted around inside with her hands for the armholes. Maggie held the sleeves out while first one small arm and then the other pushed through.

The dress was too long; its hem came down to her ankles, but the little girl pulled up the waist and spun around, just as Maggie had done exactly one year ago today, so that the skirt ballooned out like a parasol.

"Tell us," the older girl said. She was sitting on the bed, pressed up against Maggie's side, and sometimes she played with Maggie's long, soft hair.

Maggie began to tell them. She told about how she and her aunts had gotten the parlor ready, with the dishes set out on a table and the chairs arranged in a circle. She told about what Aunt Harriet and Aunt Lillian wore and about how they had surprised her with a dress of her own, the first new dress she had been given for as long as she could remember. She told about how the two aunts had baked all the cookies with wheat germ and filled the candy bowls with things like raw cauliflower and celery hearts. She told them, in fact, everything that happened up to the moment the first doorbell rang, but she couldn't tell them anything beyond that because, as it turned out, the party she attended that day—a year ago, May fourteenth—was not the same one for which her aunts had bought her the dress, and it didn't take place in their parlor.

CHAPTER EIGHTEEN

꧁꧂

For a long while she held very still, blinking into the strange light, staring at the scene before her, trying to make sense out of it all. What was it, anyway? Some kid's playroom or what? She was surrounded by pieces of furniture, but it was all *knee high*: a table set with small flowered dishes, two armchairs, a sofa, an iron stove, a cabinet, a couple of beds, a chest. Two old dolls were propped up on chairs at the table. Whose were they?

Everything had the air of being suddenly abandoned. Somebody, just moments before, had been playing here, had arranged the dolls at the table, had given them voices, had called Maggie's name, had broken a cup, had cried out, "At last!" when Maggie flung aside the curtain, and then had gone. Maggie looked around for some exit, some hiding place. There were no doors, and the window was high above the ground. Through the raging snowflakes she could see, far, far below—three stories maybe—the front steps of the house, with the stone urns, tiny now and mounded high with snow, like ice cream cones.

There was an alcove in one wall, but it was only as high as her hip, and it held a washtub with a washboard, a broom, a mop, and a dustpan—nothing more. She examined the front of the wardrobe that served as one wall of the little room. Maybe someone was inside. She pressed her ear against its front door, listening, listening, but she heard nothing, and finally she turned the latch. The interior was dark and empty and smelled of old wood.

She turned again to the dolls, with their china faces webbed with cracks. One was dressed in woman's clothing, one in man's, and Maggie looked from one to the other, taking in their finely traced eyebrows, their brightly outlined lips, their closed ears. The woman doll wore a dark print dress, long and full, with a frill of lace flaring like a flower vase at each wrist. A white cotton cap was pinned to the patch of red matting that covered her china scalp, and a string of beads hung at her neck. One china hand lay stiffly on the lid of the china teapot, the other rested on a little shawl that served as tablecloth. On her feet were leather boots with rows of tiny buttons, and on the floor beneath her lay a scattering of china fragments.

The man doll had short red hair, painted side-whiskers, a heavy suit of clothes, and a ruffled collar at his chin. An oblong of yellow newsprint was propped between his outstretched hands. He, too, wore black buttoned boots, and at his feet, in a straw basket, a china dog lay curled on a pillow of faded red velvet.

Who owned them? Who had dressed them? spoken for them? seated them in their chairs? Who? Maggie stepped back into the darkness on the other side of the wardrobe and peered at the large gowned shapes. Someone, maybe, was inside one of them, waiting. Slowly, silencing her shoes against the floor, she walked toward them. She could snatch off their white coverings, one after another, and . . .

Suddenly there was a rustling from the doll room, and a voice, the familiar voice of the walls and the trees, spoke aloud. "NOW WE MAY BEGIN!" and Maggie rushed back in.

"She's here at last." The voice came—could that be?—from the woman doll—from inside her head or something, because her lips didn't move, but she was *speaking,* saying real words—a *doll.* At the same moment, her china hand, suddenly alive, began to grasp the handle of the teapot and to lift it from the table. Maggie shrank back. What was going on? "Timothy John," the doll said, or seemed to say, "put down your paper. It's Maggie. She's here."

And then the man doll also, with some deep interior grindings and creakings, began to move, stirring in his chair and slowly lowering the scrap of newsprint to his knee. Maggie's hands grew cold. "Ah, there you are, Maggie," he said, in the voice that she had come to know over the months as "the man's." "I was afraid you had lost your way. It must be nearly teatime, isn't it?" and he turned slowly to face the other doll.

"It's past," the woman doll answered.

"It can't be past," he answered, "if it hasn't begun," and by bending forward at the waist and straightening first one leg and then the other, he rose from his chair.

Maggie edged back to the wardrobe.

"The trouble is," the woman doll said, leaning over the table, "we can't have tea at all. There is no cup at this place," and she tapped her hand on the edge of the table. "A teacup is a very important thing at teatime. It keeps the tea from being poured into the saucer."

"You do have a cup," the man doll corrected her. "It is lying next to your shoe."

The woman doll bent down to inspect the hill of china fragments at her feet. "That is true," she agreed, "although it seems a bit rearranged."

"That's because you broke it," the man doll told her.

"I didn't break it," she answered. "I only dropped it. It broke itself when it hit the floor."

"Maybe we should drop the others," the man doll suggested, "so that they will all match."

"But they might not break in the same way," the woman doll said, "and then none of them would match. I think Maggie should sweep this one up and choose another from the shelf. Maggie"—and she slowly turned her body in Maggie's direction—"would you mind getting the broom?"

Maggie felt as though she had been suddenly picked out of an audience and addressed by a puppet on a stage. Her face flamed and she pressed her back against the wardrobe.

"The broom is right there," the man doll said, also addressing her, and he stretched his arm toward the little alcove where a rush broom stood against the wall. Above it a red dustpan with a painted flower on its tray hung from a hook. "I wonder," he said to his doll companion, "how did people sweep up teacups before there were brooms?"

"There were no teacups before there were brooms," she replied. "The teacup was invented *because* of the broom. To give the broom something to do."

Maggie kept her eyes fixed firmly on the two dolls. If need be, she could turn around in a second and fly back to her room, but for now she waited and watched. The man doll had resumed his seat and was holding out the strip of newsprint in front of his face. The woman doll's hand was poised once again on the teapot. Neither doll moved, and Maggie wondered if maybe, as in puppet shows, the performance had come to an end. Would a curtain come down? Should she clap? Maybe they needed winding, and she put her hand out an inch, two inches.

"Come, Maggie," the man doll suddenly said, lowering his bit of newspaper. "Miss Christabel is waiting."

Miss Christabel? That was the other doll's name? Maggie looked again at its webbed china face. Miss Christabel. An apt name: fragile, like a crystal bell.

"Come," the woman doll said. "Before the water boils away."

What water? What was this, anyway? Who are you? she wanted to ask. *What* are you? But the words only lay in her throat, and again she watched as though the two dolls were puppets in a theater.

Suddenly she heard a new noise—a soft grumbling, like a gentle snore, issuing from the floor. The man doll lowered his arm. "Juniper is hungry for his tea," he said, and, slowly bending from the waist, he reached down to the basket at his feet and raised the china dog to his lap.

Maggie had seen china animals like that on knickknack shelves—molded hollow figures with shiny glaze, painted whiskers, and a hole underneath where your finger would fit. The dog on the doll's lap had a black patch across its head and another at the end of its tail. There was a touch of pink inside each ear and a blue dot for each eye. Its front paws held a red ball, chipped like a polished fingernail.

"Juniper," the man doll said, stroking the dog's back with the edge of his china hand, "soon we'll have our tea, and then we'll all go out to the garden."

The garden. Did these dolls visit her garden? Did they somehow manage to slip downstairs without being noticed and go outside? Had they all along been spying on her from some hidden corner as she sat, seemingly alone, under the birches? If she had looked in just the right place, could she have caught sight of a china hand among the rosebushes or a tiny black boot under a shrub?

"Maggie will want to see the roses," the man doll said, continuing to address the dog. "They are looking especially bright today." The snow was still hurtling past the little window, and there were no roses; the bushes outside had been bare for several weeks and wrapped in burlap shawls. Or was there some other garden where roses still bloomed?

"But we can't go to the garden," the woman doll said, "until we have tea. And we can't have tea until there's a new cup. And we can't have a new cup until the old one is swept away, because I get splinters in my shoe every time I move."

The tea table was set for three. The third place would be for the little dog, Maggie decided. Or was there a third doll? She swept her eye around the little room, in search of another china head, a baby head, maybe, but there was nothing besides the doll furniture, and she began inspecting it piece by piece: two canopied beds; a china cabinet with rows of doll dishes stacked in little pyramids; a sofa with dents in the pillows where two small heads had rested; a clothes chest with carved handles at either end; a stove like the ones in old-fashioned calendar scenes—black and square with a high shelf holding a row of canisters and a bread box. All in all, it was a room that was just right for the two china dolls—or three. A nice room. The Backwoods Girls would love it.

"Choose a cup to match the saucer, Maggie," the man doll said. "We can't have you taking your tea out of an odd set."

The third setting was for her? She was supposed to join them at the table? The dolls were leaning forward now, turning their faces toward her. They were just a couple of old dolls, she told herself, dumb old dolls, and yet, crazily, they were waiting for her to move, to speak, to sweep up a little hill of fragments from the floor, to take tea with them. She turned her eyes away.

Outside, the snowflakes were thinning out. A distant crow sailed past, and she listened to its caw, wishing somehow that it would fly to the window and interrupt, with some urgent message, this strange moment when two dolls waited for her to follow their command.

But the crow flew out of view, and the window showed nothing but a square of floating flakes, limp as lettuce shreds. "Well, Maggie?" the man doll said. They were expecting her to answer them, to obey them even—a couple of dolls less than two feet tall and a knickknack dog she could hold aloft like a thimble on the tip of her finger.

Just a short while ago she had expected to find two nice strangers and a dog welcoming her excitedly to their special place behind the schoolroom door. Before that, over the weeks when she listened to the voices, she had created visions of a wonderful room with a stove and a kettle and tea things and a real dog scratching at the door. And all along, the voices had belonged only to a couple of old dolls and a china animal in a jumble of toy furniture. There wasn't even a door.

"Maggie," the man doll said. "Miss Christabel's shoe keeps getting bits of teacup in its sole." His smile remained sweet and patient as he turned toward her.

Okay, then, she would answer them, and she took a long breath. She should have cleared her throat, too, because when at last she did speak, her voice came out cracked.

"I don't play with dolls," she got out.

CHAPTER NINETEEN

❧

"I don't play with dolls," she repeated, loudly this time—too loudly for so small a space—in case they hadn't heard.

The man doll nodded his smiling face. "Then we must be remarkably alike," he said. "*I* don't play with dolls. Every morning, in fact, the first thing I do is not play with dolls. Sometimes, late into the day as well," he added, "although by evening I am busy not doing other things. Playing the violin, for instance, or shining shoes. Do you also not play the violin?"

Maggie looked from one doll to the other as they sat in their little chairs. "What are you?" she finally whispered.

"Not *what*," the man doll replied. "*How*, you're supposed to say. *How* are you."

"No, I mean *what*. *Who*. Who are you?"

The man doll rose. "I am Timothy John," he said. Stiffly he bent from the waist, forming a right angle and at the same time offering Maggie his hand. "And this is Miss Christabel. She is my wife."

"That's not what I mean," Maggie answered, ignoring the hand. "I mean, what are you doing here?"

"Doing here? But just a moment ago you were interested in what we *weren't* doing here. I must think. Well, Miss Christabel is collecting teacup splinters in her shoe, for one, and I am offering you my hand. But not to keep, mind you. I would like it back when you are through shaking it."

"But how come you look like that?"

"Like what?"

"Like *that*. You know. Like whatever it is you're made of. China or something."

"That seems a strange question. Most people look like what they're made of. You do yourself." He continued to lean forward with his hand extended, and Maggie held her place at the window.

"Timothy John is waiting to shake your hand," the woman doll urged, but Maggie turned away.

Outside, far, far below, two dark figures, small as crows, were picking their way across the snowy walk toward the house. Aunt Lillian and Aunt Harriet were returning from wherever they had gone, and in a moment they would be inside. Funny to think of them down there, doing all their usual things, dusting and writing and gliding about on their silent wheels, while all the time she was up here, *here*, in this crazy place, in a secret room they knew nothing about with two creatures they had never seen.

A secret room. She turned back to study once more the little chairs and table and the kettle on the stove. It was like a house, almost; like the make-believe house she had laid out with sticks on the grass under the birches, except this one had real furniture in it, and . . .

"How do you do," the man doll said now, his hand still reaching toward her.

. . . and people, sort of. A little house with furniture and people. She stared at the doll hand with its unseparated fingers and pink oval nails. What would it feel like, she wondered: warm and alive, like her own—or cold as a teacup? She put her hand out a short distance, but withdrew it. It was just a doll's hand after all. It was stupid to shake hands with a doll.

The two aunts were no longer on the front walk. Only their footprints, like a caravan of insects, patterned the snow, and from somewhere she heard the muffled sound of a door slamming shut. Pretty soon they would begin to move around downstairs, snapping open the writing desk, snapping it shut, snapping open their mouths, snapping them shut, calling aloud: Maggie! your bed is unmade. Maggie! you have littered your room. Maggie! your breakfast is untouched. Maggie

[164]

this, Maggie that, wondering where she was, never guessing.

"When you have shaken Timothy John's hand," the woman doll persisted, "you may get the broom." Maggie turned her eyes back to the little room. To the little house with people. With a mother and a father, sort of. And a dog. And three places at the table—one for her. She could be the little girl. "The teacup is still at my foot," the woman doll added.

The man doll peered under the table. "Luckily," he said, "there are still a great many places where the teacup is *not*."

"Yes, but my foot doesn't happen to be in any of them."

Maggie took a deep breath and leaned down. Slowly, slowly, she put her arm out, drew it in, put it out again, and in a quick instant closed her fingers around the small china hand. It was cold and smooth as a stone, and she pulled back as though she had touched a hot coal.

"Well!" the woman doll exclaimed with a sigh that came, like the words she spoke, from somewhere inside her head. "Now you belong. How very nice. Just sweep up the china bits and we can have our tea."

"No I don't," Maggie said. "I don't belong to anything," but she took a step forward, and then another and another, and, without looking at either doll, advanced to the little alcove, where she seized the broom in one hand and the dustpan in the other and in one swift movement swept the broken pieces into the pail.

"Ah," said Miss Christabel. "Now there's a place for my foot to rest. Wasn't that nicely done, Timothy John? Now choose your cup," and Maggie, still not looking at either doll, examined the stack of cups until she found one with the same cluster of flowers that decorated the saucer at her place on the table. "It has a crack," she said, thrusting it in front of the woman doll's face.

Miss Christabel leaned over to peer at it. "So it does," she agreed. "And a nice one, too. Like a little vine. Now bring the kettle, and mind your fingers; it will be hot."

Maggie pressed her palm against the side of the kettle on the stove. "It's cold," she said. "Cold as ice. And besides," she added, looking inside, "it's empty. Nothing's in it." She swung the kettle around her head and held it upside down. "See?"

"Look out!" both dolls cried at once. "You'll spill!" and Maggie jumped back, but nothing came out of the spout at all.

"Bring it to the table," Timothy John said. "And hold it right side up. The water will stay inside better that way."

"There isn't any water," Maggie said, but she carried it right side up anyway, and dropped it on the table. The teapot was empty, too, she noticed, and so were the sugar bowl and the creamer.

"Fill the teapot now," Timothy John said.

She remembered a myth or a fairy tale about an empty pitcher that poured wine or something every time it was tipped over a bowl. Maybe this kettle was magic like that. Maybe hot water would really bubble from its spout and tea leaves would spring to life in the teapot. With both hands she tilted the kettle and watched expectantly, but nothing came out at all, and the teapot remained empty and cold. "There's nothing in it," she shouted, slamming it on the table.

"Slowly," Miss Christabel cautioned. "Don't splash the tablecloth."

"And don't forget the tea cozy," Timothy John added.

The what? Maggie stared at him.

"Over here," and Timothy John nodded at a little crocheted hat on the table. Maggie turned it over in her hands a few times and finally pulled it over Miss Christabel's head.

"Mercy!" exclaimed Miss Christabel.

"On the teapot," Timothy John corrected, and Maggie crammed it on the empty china pot. A hat for a teapot?

"That will keep the heat inside," Miss Christabel explained.

"If the heat gets out," Timothy John added, "it gets mixed up with the cold, and nobody can find it."

"Oh, and the lid of the bread tin is stuck, Maggie," Miss Christabel said. "See if you can pry it off." She pointed to the shelf over the stove.

The bread box rattled when Maggie reached it down, and she found three slabs inside. "They're wood," she said, holding them up for the dolls to see.

"Bring them to the table," Timothy John said.

"Wooden bread," and Maggie dropped them one by one on the tablecloth. "With butter painted on."

"They belong on a plate," Miss Christabel corrected her. "And overlap them so they won't fall off. The tea must be ready by now. I can smell it," and she brought her hands to her cup, holding it out for Maggie to fill.

"It is our best tea," Timothy John commented. "Its vapors will put curls in your hair. Did you know that? And try the bread, too. It will fatten your wrists."

The two dolls raised their teacups and their bread to their lips, first one and then the other, and Maggie listened to the little clicks—china to china and china to wood. After a long while she lifted her own teacup and sniffed at it. "It doesn't have any vapors," she said, lowering it again. "It doesn't smell at all," and after another long moment she put the tip of her tongue to the wooden crust. "It tastes like wood," she said, dropping it back on the table, but quietly, turning aside, she touched the hank of hair at her cheek, testing it, and she checked her lower arm. Her hair was stiff and moist as always, and her wrist remained thin and full of bones, like the neck of a chicken.

Miss Christabel put her saucer next to the dog's basket,

and he growled softly, as a cat purrs. "Have some tea, Juniper," she said. "And then we will walk to the garden. It seems an especially nice day for the garden, doesn't it, Timothy John?"

"Lovely," he answered.

"It's snowing," Maggie said.

"Not in the garden," Timothy John answered.

"Where is it?" she asked.

"Where is it snowing? But you already know that."

"No, where is the *garden*?"

"Ah, the garden. The garden is that place which is surrounded by everything that *isn't* garden. It is also where the roses grow."

"But first we must tidy up," Miss Christabel said, and she put everything where it had been when Maggie had first entered this room an hour, two hours, an age ago.

"Now then!" Timothy John removed a small top hat from a hook on the wall and placed it on his head. Next he took up the little scrap of newspaper and hung a small cane over his jointed wrist. "Garden time," he announced, and he picked Juniper up in his basket.

"Garden time," Miss Christabel repeated, and she slipped her arm through the handle of the kettle.

Maggie said nothing at all, but followed the two dolls first with her eye and then with shortened steps as they rounded the table and worked their way, inch by inch, to the end of

[169]

the wall, around the far corner, and along a narrow corridor, toward—what? Maggie couldn't tell, but she looked over her shoulder once, twice, to memorize the way back to the room with the little table and chairs, the sofa with the dented pillows, and the teapot that held no tea.

CHAPTER TWENTY

❧

The two dolls paused along the way and sat down to rest on a pair of knee-high wicker armchairs in some far region of the attic. Maggie leaned against the wall and waited, wondering how long it would take, at this rate, to reach the outdoors. What if they didn't get there until after dark? What if the garden were at the end of some tunnel whose mouth she would never find again? She shifted against the wall and looked around.

A block of light came in from a high window, but there was little to see: a couple of chairs, a fluff of dust, a wall papered in a faded print. She was eager to move on, and her eye searched for the doorway or turning that would take them on their way.

At last Timothy John stirred in his chair. "Well, now," he said, and Maggie straightened up, but he only leaned over to set Juniper's basket on the floor. "Well, now," he repeated, and he raised the little scrap of newsprint to his face, studying it for a long while. "I see in the paper," he said carefully, "that there's been a fire. 'Two Lost in Fire,' it says."

Miss Christabel turned to face him from her chair.

"Pity," she said, and then, after a moment, "Two lost in fire. Read it to me, Timothy John."

Timothy John turned the paper this way and that until it caught the light coming in from the high window. " 'Washtub for Sale,' " he began.

"No. Read about the fire."

" 'Two Lost in Fire,' " he repeated. "That's in big letters. " 'Fire broke out suddenly in the barn at . . .' That's all there is," he apologized.

Maggie looked over at the torn newsprint and saw on one side an advertisement with a picture of an old-fashioned washtub, and on the other the headline Timothy John had just read. At the top corner was a portion of a date, and Maggie leaned closer to read it: Wednesday, May 14, 18 something. The rest was torn away.

"Pity," Miss Christabel repeated. "Two lost in fire. Two what, I wonder."

"It doesn't say," Timothy John answered. "Gloves, maybe. Maybe somebody lost two gloves in the fire. Gloves come in twos, and people are always losing them, even when there is no fire."

"That could be. Wouldn't that be a shame, though. Imagine losing two gloves and not being able to find them in all that smoke. I hope they were from the same pair."

Timothy John put the paper under his arm and began to rise. "Well," he said, and Maggie prepared to continue their trip to the garden, but he only moved Juniper's basket again, this time placing it in the square of light that lay on the floor like a white rug. "Sit down a bit, Maggie," he said, settling himself back in the wicker chair. "You must be tired after all that walking."

"When are we going to the garden?" she asked, not moving.

Timothy John turned his smiling face up to her. "What?" he asked.

"The garden. When are we going there?"

Miss Christabel turned in her chair. "We're not going there," she said.

"But I thought you said that's where we were going," Maggie insisted, turning to Timothy John. "You even put on your hat and everything."

"We can't be going to the garden," he answered, "when we are already there."

Maggie stared at him. Already there? This was the garden? *This?*

"It is especially lovely today," Timothy John went on, and he pushed his chair to the patch of light next to Juniper's basket. "The sun feels good on a day like this," he said, sitting down and putting his face to the thin white rays coming through the window.

"The roses are especially nice, too," Miss Christabel said. "Maggie, turn your face to the roses. They will redden your cheek, see if they don't."

"See if they *do*," Timothy John corrected.

Maggie looked at both dolls. "What roses?" she asked, her voice louder than she expected.

"All of them," Timothy John answered. "This one and this one and this one." He pointed his cane to the wall, and Maggie saw now, printed on its peeling paper, a tangle of faded flowers winding among pale trellises. These were the roses? *Wall*paper? She looked back at the dolls.

"They need watering," Miss Christabel observed. "Maggie, give them a good sprinkling so they don't droop."

"And don't forget the little ones," Timothy John added, focusing his painted eyes on the papered wall. "Here's one that looks especially thirsty," and he touched his cane to a pattern near the floor molding where everything but a few traces of pink had rubbed away.

Maggie looked at the wallpaper. "That's what you call a garden? You want me to water *that*?"

"Of course," Miss Christabel replied. "Before they wilt,"

and she turned to examine the papered wall. "I can't think what I would do without my roses," she remarked contentedly. "They brighten my life."

"What with?" Maggie asked.

"With happiness," Miss Christabel answered.

"What should I *water* them with?"

"With water," and Miss Christabel held out the kettle. "And don't forget the little buds. Hurry," she urged, when Maggie still did not move.

Maggie stared at both dolls. "That's dumb," she finally said. "That's the dumbest thing I ever heard. Watering *wallpaper*."

"You may begin with these," Timothy John said, and he pointed his cane at the faded patch.

"Dumb," Maggie repeated. "And anyway," she added, suddenly remembering something, "you can't water the roses with that kettle. It's got hot water in it. It's *hot,* remember?"

Timothy John stared at her. "Maggie," he said patiently, "that's the *tea* water you're thinking of. There's *rose* water in the kettle now."

"There's *nothing* in the kettle now," Maggie answered back. "See?" She seized the kettle and held it upside down over the floor.

"Hold it closer to the roots," Timothy John admonished her. "The roots are the throat of the plant."

Maggie lowered her arm.

The roots are the throat of the plant. What a strange spectacle that made: every stem ending, underground, in a soft, pink, gummy cavity, opening, closing, opening, closing, taking large drafts of water in steady, thirsty gulps, and sending them . . . where? Up, instead of down. And in this case, up a papered wall, except there wasn't any water to gulp in the first place.

She dropped the kettle to the floor. "They don't *have* roots," she shouted. "These aren't real roses. They're wallpaper. It's stupid to water wallpaper roses, and anyway there's no water in this kettle, hot *or* cold, and there's no tea in that teapot either, and no sugar in the sugar bowl, and no milk in the pitcher, and that's not real bread—it's just pieces of wood." Her voice had risen even more. "And you're just a couple of old dolls." She stopped. Both Timothy John and Miss Christabel rose from their chairs and were advancing toward her, Timothy John with his cane clutched in his hand.

Maggie stepped back against the flowered wall and held her breath, feeling suddenly trapped—trapped in an attic room no one knew about by a pair of mechanical dolls, or whatever they were, who could—what?—kill her maybe. With a twist of his jointed wrist the man doll could hurl his cane at her, if he chose, stabbing her to death. It could have poison in its tip, and all he would have to do was scratch it against her skin. She could die up here, of blood poisoning or something, and no one would ever know. "She's run away," Aunt Harriet would decide after a day or two. "It's not surprising," Aunt Lillian would reply. "She never did belong here. She was a difficult child." *Was*, they would say. In a few days' time they would clear out her room, never dreaming that her body lay only a few dozen yards away, crumpled alongside the peeling roses on a papered wall.

The two dolls drew nearer and Maggie's stomach grew watery. In the next moment she swung her foot out and sent both dolls sprawling across the room. The garden. Whatever it was. With their arms outstretched and their legs straightened behind them, they looked as though they were swimming in a pool. But Timothy John's head soon struck the far wall and his body slid down to the floor, and Miss Christabel sat down hard against the wicker chair. Both continued to smile their red painted smiles, Timothy John up at the ceiling, Miss Christabel across the room at Maggie. Just under the rubbed-out patch of flowers, Juniper lay upside down, the hole in his underside exposed to view.

She crossed over to their bodies on tiptoe and bent down to look at them. A long crack, clean as a wire, ran across Timothy John's forehead, and one of Miss Christabel's legs jutted out at a crazy angle from the hem of her skirt. Juniper was missing an ear. Maggie touched the man doll's body with the toe of her shoe, as though she were testing a dead bird, but he didn't stir. Neither doll stirred.

Maybe she had broken them for good. Maybe she could pick them up now and hold them upside down. She could even take them apart, if she liked, and see what was inside. Maybe she would find, in the hollow of each body, some tiny mechanism, like the works of a music box, that had made them walk and talk or purr like a cat.

Timothy John's body shifted suddenly on the floor, and he began to speak. "I think," he said, his eyes still on the ceiling, "she is the wrong one after all."

"The wrong one," Miss Christabel repeated from the legs of the chair. "It seems odd, though. She seemed so right."

"We will have to wait for another."

"It is a pity," Miss Christabel sighed. "We waited so long. It might be decades before another one came." Her voice faded on the last words and ran down, like a phonograph suddenly shut off.

After that neither doll spoke.

"I don't care!" Maggie shouted into the stillness. "I don't want to be the right one. You're just a couple of old dolls." She began edging away, retreating along the wall, along the narrow corridor, past the little room, around the wardrobe, and through the clusters of shrouded furniture in the attic until she reached the top of the stairs that would take her back to the empty room. "I don't play with dolls!" she called back into the darkness.

There came no answer, and it wasn't until she had felt her way down to the bottom of the steps that she heard anything at all: the voices first of Aunt Lillian and then of Aunt Harriet. "Maggie! Where are you?"

CHAPTER TWENTY-ONE

❧

Maggie was alone in the kitchen, polishing silverware. "Ingesting silver tarnish is dangerous to the system," Aunt Lillian had said, and she had sat Maggie down with a jar of polish, a heap of rags, and the contents of the silver drawer laid out in squadrons across the table. The tablespoons had nice round surfaces, and Maggie began with them, spreading on thick pink paste and rubbing until the rag turned black and her finger, poking through, turned black too. Then she dropped each spoon into a pail of water and polished it until it gleamed and she could see her face, upside down, in its hollow.

The January light entered the window reluctantly, casting its meager glow in a narrow panel across the table. Maggie had to bring the spoon closer and closer to her face in order to see into it, so close finally that her features flipped right side up and all she could see was the bulb of her nose. She sat and stared at its pink flesh until her breath steamed it over.

Silence had settled down on the house once again. Like a fog, it filled the corners, slipped behind the curtains, rose from the rugs, and crept under the covers at night when Maggie went to bed. Everything was as it had been during her first days at Adelphi Hills, before the voices. Aunt Harriet and Aunt Lillian moved about from room to room on their silent wheels. Sometimes they went out, but Maggie never knew where they went, or when, even. Often it wasn't until she saw their rubber galoshes lying in a pool of slush in the front hall that she knew they had gone out at all.

Maggie, too, moved from room to room, although she wasn't allowed to enter most of them. She would slip upstairs after school and wander through the hallway, opening doors, fingering a hairbrush or a string of beads, returning to the hallway with its dark silent walls.

Sometimes she missed the voices. Once she thought she heard them, and she flung open her bedroom door, but it was only Aunt Harriet moving slowly at the other end of the corridor, her sleeves whispering against her dress as she dusted the moldings. It didn't matter; the voices just belonged to some dumb dolls anyway. Besides, the dolls didn't want her either. She wasn't the right one.

Who would have been? she wondered. Someone, probably, who would have poured their pretend tea and nibbled their wooden bread and politely watered their wallpaper roses and sat in their make-believe garden saying all the right things. Someone nice.

Sometimes the Backwoods Girls came to visit. "This is a light," she said, pausing between doorways in the long corridor. "Ooh, how wonderful," they answered, as she pulled on the cord and created a small disk of orange at the edge of her feet. But she could find nothing else to show them, and they soon retreated to their haunts in the woods.

Uncle Morris came once. "We should visit the roses," he said, and she looked up at him sharply. What roses? But he meant the ones outside in the garden. "Roses tend to die in the winter. Not from the frost, as everyone thinks, but from boredom. Imagine sitting out in a garden all winter long with not even a magazine to look at. Come on, we'll cheer them up," and he led her outside. They stood awhile in the snow, facing a row of rose bushes wrapped against the wind in their burlap shawls. "I always felt it to be a great mistake," he said, "to have winter in January when it is so cold. They should have it in July when we can all go out and enjoy it." He touched one of the burlap wrappings with the silver knob of his walking stick. "Roses wear these blankets to keep their throats from getting sore," he said, and again she looked up at him. The dolls had said something like that. Throats of the plant. "What throats?" she asked, but he only answered, "The ones with all those tonsils. Do you know what rose tonsils are, Maggie?" She didn't bother to listen to the rest.

She stuck her finger into the silver polish. It was lovely and pink and it made big creamy smears on the enameled kitchen table like finger paint. She rippled it into a mountain, a cloud, a fat pink sun with rays. "Look," she said to the Backwoods Girls. "This is magic paint. I can write in it with my finger. Here's my initial," and she traced out an *M* in curly script.

"Ooh, how wonderful. Write my letter, too. Write *E* for Elizabeth."

"All right, but don't shout. Here's K for Kate. Here's E for Elizabeth. M for Mary. H for Helen. A for Anne. And T.J. for you can't guess."

"Who's T.J.?"

"Never mind."

"Tell us, tell us. Who is it?"

"This person I know."

"Who?"

"None of your business." She wiped the initials away with her fist. "Somebody. Nobody."

The silence continued. Did the dolls still speak to each other, she wondered, even though they no longer spoke to her? Had they picked themselves up, after she had left, and hobbled somehow to the tea table, where they were now lifting the kettle and clicking their painted lips against the edges of the wooden bread? Were they speaking about her? Or had they fallen silent for good—for good, that is, until someone else, the right one, came along, decades from now? She could go up and see. She wouldn't have to stay, and she wouldn't even let them see her. If they *could* see. She could just stand and listen for a minute, two minutes, and then come back downstairs. Not that it mattered.

Everything was as she had left it: the little chairs around the table, the sofa, the china cabinet, the beds, the broom in its corner. Slowly she made her way past the room and along the wall that led to the place with the wallpaper—the garden.

The two dolls and the dog were lying where they had fallen—Miss Christabel half sitting, half reclining against the wicker chair, her flowered skirt flat where her knee should have been; Timothy John against the wall; and Juniper upside down beside the wallpaper roses. Maggie looked down into their china smiles, waiting for them to speak, but no sound came.

"It's me," she finally said. "Maggie. I was the one who

was here. Do you remember? I just wanted to see if you were still here or what." Neither doll moved.

It doesn't matter. She shrugged. They're just dolls. "I just came to find out if you were still here," she repeated. "I have to go now."

But she didn't go. With the edge of her toe she lifted Miss Christabel's skirt. The little china leg was separated at the knee, and Maggie bent down to pick up the broken end. Two little holes at one end marked the point where a pin had been fitted, or a wire. "Where is it?" she asked, lifting Miss Christabel's body and shaking out her dress. "Where's the little wire thing that your knee is attached to?" She knocked over one wicker chair, the other, and there in the dust lay a tiny pink-and-white chip. "Hey, here's your ear," she said to Juniper. "Look, here's the ear that came off. Here's where it goes," and she fitted it to the dog's head.

She could fix it, maybe. With the paste in her desk drawer. She could fix the dolls, too, even. They still wouldn't talk or move, because she wasn't the right one, but she could make them look the way they had before she had kicked them. She could fix them up and then leave them here. For the right one.

"Wait for me," she said, slipping Miss Christabel's leg into her pocket. "Wait. I'll be back. In a little while."

CHAPTER TWENTY-TWO

A hairpin, she thought, soundlessly sliding open the top drawer of the bureau and lifting the lids of a dozen lacquered boxes that lay inside. A skinny hairpin, and she ran her fingers through coils of pearl necklaces, tangles of earrings, clusters of golden safety pins, slippery heaps of buttons. A nice skinny hairpin, and she stirred a dish of rings.

"Maggie!"

"Maggie!"

The two voices came not quite together, but overlapping, one just behind the other. The two aunts in the doorway overlapped too, like a pair of cards: the two red queens.

"What are you doing?"

"What are you doing?"

The rings slipped from Maggie's hand and rolled across the floor.

"I was looking for a hairpin," she said.

"What are you doing in my jewelry drawer? What are you doing with my rings?" Aunt Lillian spoke alone now. "You know you are forbidden to enter these rooms."

"She's a thief," Aunt Harriet said. "She's been a thief from the moment she entered this house. She stole the clothes from her own closet."

"Gone without a trace," said Aunt Lillian.

"Sold them probably," said Aunt Harriet.

"I needed a hairpin."

"A hairpin!" Aunt Lillian sniffed. "With your hand in the ring box?"

"I was looking behind it. For a hairpin."

"A hairpin!" Aunt Harriet repeated. "For that hair?"

"No," Maggie said. "I needed it. To fix something. I—"

"Harriet," Aunt Lillian broke in, "she has something else in her pocket! She's already stolen something."

"What is it? Take it from her."

"It's a piece of china. It's a doll's leg or something." She held up Miss Christabel's leg with the little buttoned boot. "I wonder where she got it."

"From the rubbish heap, by the looks of it. Throw it out, Lillian. It's covered with germs."

"Disgusting," Aunt Lillian said. She crossed the room and

dropped Miss Christabel's leg, boot and all, into the waste-basket, where it landed with a small swish on a heap of paper scraps.

"No!" Maggie cried, surprised at the strength of her voice. "Give that back. It's Miss Chr . . . It's *mine!*" and in the next moment she dived toward the wastebasket, but a hard hand dug into each of her shoulders, and she was marched down the hall into her own room.

Aunt Lillian ruffled through Maggie's dresser drawers, stir-ring up the underwear and the tangle of socks, while Aunt Harriet slid the hangers, one after the other, along the closet pole. "Stole her own clothes," she said again.

"I didn't take anything," Maggie protested again. "I was just looking for a hairpin."

"A hairpin," Aunt Harriet said. "For those oily strings?" They faced her from the doorway. "You will stay here until you are sent for," and they closed the door after them. Maggie could hear their whispers in the hall. "It was a mistake having her here. She will have to go," and a pang went through Maggie's ribs. For the first time she could remember, she wanted to stay where she was, and she thought of Miss Christa-bel upstairs with her dress lying flat where her leg should have been, of Timothy John with a crack in his head, and of Juniper lying a quarter of an inch away from his ear. "Wait for me," she whispered, but she didn't know if she would ever see the dolls again—or Miss Christabel's leg, even.

"Maybe I'll come back," she whispered, but the room stayed quiet and she drifted over to her bed. The deck of cards lay on the pillow, and she spread them out in front of her.

"These are cards," she said to the Backwoods Girls, who suddenly appeared in their admiring circle around the bed. She had told them about cards before, but they never remembered anything. "Here's how they work. The pictures all have names. This is King of Hearts. He's the handsomest. He's married to Queen of Hearts, and this is their boy. His name is Jack."

There were voices in the corridor again, and the Backwoods Girls vanished in an instant. Maggie pressed her ear to the door. "A hairpin!" Aunt Harriet was exclaiming. "She said she wanted a hairpin, when her hair is nothing but a mass of oily strings." Silence, more footsteps, and then someone knocking on her door.

Maggie sprang away and stood at the window, her back to the room. They were coming to tell her she had to go.

"Maggie, why is it that you always turn up in the last place I look?" They had sent Uncle Morris instead. Uncle Morris, who said nice things about her in her head and teased her with his strange jokes, was the one, after all, who would tell her she had to pack her things and leave.

"Next time I shall remember to look in the last place first, and save myself the bother of opening all those doors," he went on, and she felt his eyes on her back as she stared at the wide lawn, brown and frosty today, at the ghostly clump of birches, and at the distant bed of roses in their burlap shawls. She thought of Miss Christabel, who would now never again walk in her own garden of roses, and of Timothy John, whose head would lie forever cracked against the garden wall.

"The fact is," Uncle Morris said, "there was something I wanted to say to you." Here it came. No more jokes. First a lecture, then the news. Then good-bye. "Your aunts have told me something quite unbelievable," he began.

"I wasn't stealing," Maggie said, turning to face him at last. "I was looking for something. I needed it to fix something that broke. I don't want any of their stuff. I just had to *fix* something."

Uncle Morris continued as though she hadn't spoken at all. "They told me," he said, "that there is oil in your hair."

"I didn't want the hairpin for my hair. I wanted it to fix something."

"Oil in your hair," Uncle Morris repeated. "I find that enormously interesting. Oil is a particularly useful thing in the hair. It prevents hair rust. Do you know, Maggie, what happens to people with hair rust?"

She returned her gaze to the garden. How long was it going to *take* him?

"They wake up suddenly one day," he went on, "to discover that their heads are covered with a fine orange powder that settles in little streams over their ears and clogs the tub when they take a bath. It is a dreadful thing. The first sign is a faint creak, like an aging door hinge. What a fortunate thing that you will never know the terror of hair creak. After that, it is only a matter of days before rust sets in and the tubs clog."

He was at her side now, and he had something white in his hand—a letter, maybe. He was going to tell her in writing that she had to leave. "I didn't want the hairpin for my hair," she said again. "I wanted it to fix something. I wasn't stealing their rings."

"Now I'm getting to the important part," Uncle Morris said, and Maggie felt a thump inside her ribs. "Could I borrow a small amount of your hair oil? It doesn't have to be much. Just enough to touch up some tiny creaks I heard this morning when I combed my hair." It wasn't a letter in his hand, it was a handkerchief, and he was reaching out with it to the ends of her hair, but she pulled away.

"I don't have oily hair!" she shouted. "And I wasn't stealing anything. And if you're going to send me away, tell me now!" She turned to him again, and found him looking down at her, puzzled and serious.

"Then Harriet was wrong," he said. "She insisted you had oily hair. I will have to order my hair oil from the catalog instead," and he was gone.

It wasn't until the door had closed behind him and Maggie

could no longer hear his footsteps along the corridor that she noticed that he had dropped his handkerchief on her bed—a white folded cloth with a blue M embroidered in one corner. She swept it off with her arm and then jumped, startled, when she heard a clatter as it hit the floor. Cautiously, she leaned down and stared. There at the edge of the bedspread lay Miss Christabel's leg, with a slender hairpin, gold and tiny, stuck through its china knee.

Voices rose in the hallway again—Aunt Harriet's, Aunt Lillian's, Uncle Morris's, Aunt Harriet's again. Don't make me go, Maggie said, clutching the china leg in her palm. Don't make me go, don't make me go, and then she held still as the voices moved away.

The little leg still wore its leather boot with the rows of tiny buttons, and Maggie tried to stand it up on the window seat, but it fell over. Does it feel? Maggie wondered. If I press it, will it wake up Miss Christabel in her chair and make her cry out? She gave its shin an experimental dig with her fingernail, but no cry came through the walls.

Voices again, downstairs this time, and a door closing: Uncle Morris going home. In a minute, two minutes, the aunts would come up, tell her to pack her things; she would have to go. She leaned against the wall, waiting for the step outside the door, but everything remained still, and the birches grew gray and then black outside her window.

Maggie sat on the window seat, stroking the little china leg with her finger, for a long time—how long she couldn't tell—but her room was nearly dark when from the wall— or the curtain, or the window seat—she heard, in a sudden burst of words, "MAGGIE! COME BACK! AND BRING SOME LINIMENT!"

CHAPTER TWENTY-THREE

❧❦❧

"I couldn't come back right away," Maggie explained breathlessly. "I got put in my room because I was looking for a hairpin to fix this leg, and they thought I was stealing their rings and they were going to send me away, but then Uncle Morris came and gave me a hairpin and told them to let me stay and now I can fix all of you up." She stopped. Did the dolls know who "they" were? Did they know Uncle Morris? Did they already know everything that had happened? "Did you know where I was all that time?" she asked.

Miss Christabel sat unmoving against her chair, and Timothy John continued to stare across the room from the wall. Juniper and his ear lay side by side in the little straw basket. None of them moved. Could she have been mistaken? Maybe they hadn't called her after all. Maybe she was still the wrong one. "Hey, can you hear me?" she asked.

A long silence followed. She slowly put down the things she had brought with her: the wired leg, the pink rag, the little jar of paste. "I brought all this stuff," she said. "To fix you with. I thought you wanted me back. I thought you were waiting for me all that time, and that's why you called. I thought . . ."

Timothy John slowly turned his head. "All what time?" he asked.

Maggie's heart raced and she felt a trembling in her fingers. "All the time I was downstairs," she said, "and they wouldn't let me out."

"But that was *your* time," Timothy John answered. "Not mine. Or Miss Christabel's."

Slowly Miss Christabel moved the toe of her one remaining leg. "Maggie," she said, "do you have my other shoe? I believe I left my leg in it by mistake."

"Did you bring the liniment, Maggie?" Timothy John asked. "I seem to have a sore head."

"Too much exercise," Miss Christabel said.

From inside the straw basket came the half purr of Juniper's voice.

"Okay," Maggie whispered. "Okay, I'll fix you. All of you. I'll start with you," and she turned to Timothy John. "Where does it hurt?" she asked, reaching for the pink rag and kneeling at his side. With the tip of her finger she traced the slender crack along his forehead. "Over here, or where?" She expected him to wince, or cry in pain, but he simply lay back against the wall. "Anywhere will do," he answered. "The ache is on the inside, where I can't see it."

Maggie placed the cloth across his forehead and held it down with her fingers. A small portion of pink paste began to seep from the rag, staining Timothy John's brow, and she wiped it clean with her thumb. "Quite nice," he said. "What kind of liniment are you using?"

"It's silver polish," Maggie answered.

"It doesn't look silver at all. It looks pink."

"No," Maggie corrected. "Silver is what it's *for*."

"My head is what it's for," Timothy John answered. "It's head polish."

Maggie turned to Miss Christabel. "I'll fix your leg now," she said, lifting the doll's skirt. There were two holes in the upper part that lined up with the two in the lower, and Maggie wove the hairpin through both, twisting the ends into a knot and easing the leg back and forth to set it in motion. "There," she said, standing Miss Christabel on the floor. "It's all fixed," and she leaned back on her heels to watch as Miss Christabel moved slowly toward the papered wall and back to the chair.

"It's just right," Miss Christabel said, leaning over and

lifting her skirt. "Look, Timothy John, it's just the right distance between my knee and my shoe."

Once more Juniper began to rumble from his basket.

"Juniper's been cranky since the accident."

Maggie looked at the doll carefully. "What accident?" she asked.

"When he fell."

"Fell? Fell from where?"

"From the air. Where else does one fall from? He was in the air and he fell from it."

Did they really think that? Maggie wondered. "He didn't really fall," she began to explain, but she stopped in midsentence. "I think Timothy John's head is fixed by now," she said instead, and she lifted away the rag.

"It must be," he replied. "The ache is all gone."

"Gone where?" asked Miss Christabel.

"I can't say," he replied. "I didn't see it leave."

Maggie wondered if, somehow, the scratch was gone, too, and she rubbed away the paste, caked and dry now and turning to powder beneath her finger. The crack remained as before, though, fine as a whisker, but pinker, like a scratch from a rose thorn. Slowly Timothy John lifted himself up from the floor and made his way over to the chair next to Miss Christabel. "I see by the paper," he said, lifting his bit of newsprint, "that there's been a fire."

Juniper began to growl again, and Maggie went over to his basket. "I can fix your ear, too," she said. "I brought something for it," and she unscrewed the lid of the paste jar.

"Did you bring ear polish for Juniper?" Timothy John asked.

"No, this is library paste."

"Library paste?" Timothy John replied in surprise. "For pasting libraries together?"

"No, it's for paper and china and stuff."

"That seems a strange substance to use for dog ears."

Maggie scraped off a fingernailful from the edge of the jar and applied a bit to each raw edge of china. Next she pressed the ear to Juniper's head and held both pieces in her fist, tight, tight, tight, until her palm grew hot and moist and her knuckles ached. "You have to wait until the paste dries," she explained through her fingers. "And you have to hold very still or it won't stick and your ear will fall off again and you won't be able to hear." Was that true? Did Juniper hear through his ear?

"There is a washtub for sale," Timothy John announced, turning the scrap of newspaper in his hands. "It looks like a very fine one. Could you use a washtub?" he inquired of Miss Christabel.

"I already have a washtub," she replied. "In fact, Maggie, when Juniper's ear is mended, you can help with the laundry."

The laundry. What was that supposed to mean? She thought of watering the roses with an empty kettle and sipping air from empty teacups.

Timothy John peered once again at his newspaper. "You might use a second washtub for the dog," he said to Miss Christabel, and this time there was an answering rumble from Maggie's closed fist. "There's one for sale at Streeter's, and it's guaranteed never to leak, but I can't quite make out the price," and he drew the paper close to his face.

Maggie leaned over to examine it. "That's because it's torn off," she said. "And besides, they don't sell washtubs like that anymore. That paper is from a hundred years ago or something."

Timothy John looked at the paper again. "If this is today," he said, "then this is today's paper. Besides, it says 'Washtub for Sale *Now*,' so there you are."

Maggie sighed and began to open her cramped fingers one by one, to see if Juniper's ear was holding. "It's sticking," she said, testing it with the tip of a finger. "It's really sticking. But you'll have to be careful. Don't shake your head a whole lot." That was dumb. Juniper couldn't shake his head at all.

"All of you are fixed now," she announced to Miss Christabel with her wired knee, to Timothy John with his pink scar, and to Juniper with his glued ear nestling in the warmth of her palm. She felt a sudden sense of pride. As far as she could remember she had never fixed—really fixed—anything in her life. "I made you better," she said.

"Better than whom?" Timothy John asked.

"No, I mean you're not broken anymore."

"Broken! You speak as though we were teacups."

"Come," Miss Christabel exclaimed. "It's time to do the laundry," and little by little they made their way back to the other room. "See if the water in the kettle is hot, Maggie," she urged, "and then you may begin with these bloomers."

"What are bloomers?" Maggie asked.

"These." Miss Christabel held up a small pair of long underpants gathered at each leg with a pink ribbon.

Maybe she should go now. It was stupid rubbing a whole bunch of doll clothes against a tin washboard in an empty tub and pretending they were getting washed. It was stupid doing a lot of things up here. Fixing the dolls when they were broken was okay, and straightening up a bit, too, maybe, but everything else was playing dolls. "I have to go now," she said.

Miss Christabel removed something else from the wash basket—a little square of cloth with red flowers, roses or something, embroidered into each corner. "Oh, Maggie," she said. "Do this first. It's my favorite handkerchief. I always like to have a handkerchief tucked into my sleeve. It's nice to dab at things with."

Maggie set Juniper down on the table. "I have to go," she said.

A sound came from far, far beneath the floor. A call. "Maggie!" So distant, it was only a brushstroke against her ear. *"Maggie!"* It was Aunt Lillian.

The two dolls didn't seem to hear. Miss Christabel held out the tiny handkerchief, Timothy John looked into his newspaper, and Juniper sat upright on the table.

"Maggie!" Aunt Harriet this time.

"First the handkerchief," Miss Christabel said, "and *then* the bloomers."

"Maggie!" *"Maggie!"* Both aunts together.

Maggie paused to look at Miss Christabel, her leg all nicely mended, with the tiny handkerchief in her outstretched hand. Timothy John had settled down in his chair and was reading the newspaper, just as he had been before his head got cracked, and Juniper, whole again, growled happily on the table. She had fixed them. Made them better. She was their caretaker, sort of.

"See if the water is hot yet," Miss Christabel said again.

Maggie lifted the little kettle from the iron stove and tested its bottom quickly with the flat of her hand. It was as cold as ever.

"It's hot," she said. "Scalding hot."

CHAPTER TWENTY-FOUR

Every Monday was Sharing Day in Miss Hunter's classroom. Sharing didn't mean sharing at all. It meant telling about what you did over the weekend, or holding up some great thing you brought from home, and not passing it around because you didn't want it to get ruined.

"Who has something to share?" Miss Hunter would begin, and at first no hand would go up, but finally Edwin or somebody would have something. "Here's a stamp," he would say. "I got it at this stamp show—"

"Louder," Miss Hunter would interrupt.

"Here's a stamp. I got it at this stamp show I went to with my father. It's from Morocco and it has this camel or something on it. I'm not sure—its hump is sort of pointy for a

camel. And we saw this really rare stamp that's worth about a million dollars because it was printed upside down."

Then Howard would show a real arrowhead, a cobra skin, a tiny fish kite from Japan. Where did they *get* all these things?

"Barbara? Have you something to share?" Yes. Barbara had spent the whole weekend with her cousins who were visiting from Canada, and they had gone ice-skating in the city. "Alyssa?" Alyssa had seen a horror movie and she told its whole plot. "Maggie?" Maggie would coil a wet strand of hair around her finger and let it spring loose. "Nothing again? Carolyn?"

But today Maggie had something to share.

"Maggie? Nothing again?"

No. Yes. *Yes!* I have. I have something to share. She looked around at the faces in the room. What would she tell them? That she had found two old dolls who talked and moved around like real people and set up housekeeping behind a wardrobe in the attic where they served wooden bread at a tea table and watered wallpaper roses with an empty kettle?

She returned her eyes to her desk and began tracing with her pen the grooves of the letter R that someone had carved there long ago. "Maggie, we don't write on our desks. Did you have something to share today?"

"Yes."

Glances crisscrossed the room like searchlights in the sky, targeting her body. What did she have to share?

"I visited these people I know," she began. "They live in this place that has a garden outside." Her voice sounded like some distant echo. "And they have a dog." She paused a long while, so long that Miss Hunter thought she was finished, and called on someone else. "Sharon? Did you have your hand up?" But Maggie suddenly plunged ahead. "They have all these beautiful things. They have a whole tea set painted with pansies and daisies, and I get to pour the tea and pass around the bread and butter. And there's a tea cozy, which is this thing that looks like a ski hat that you put on the teapot and it keeps the tea warm. After tea we go outside with the dog and sit in the garden. There are millions of roses climbing all over the place, and it's my job to water them.

"We all sit together in front of the roses in wicker chairs and the man reads the newspaper and we talk about what he reads. After that we feed the dog and feel the sun on our faces and smell the millions of roses. Then we go back inside. And I did their laundry for them: first, some bloomers—that's these underpants, sort of, with ribbons at the knees. . . ." From somewhere behind her came a small sound—a laugh contained in someone's throat—and then another, also small. "I washed them in the washtub and hung them on the line out in the rose garden, and then I ironed them on the tea table with this iron you have to heat on the stove, and then I folded them in a neat stack on the table the way they showed me. When I was through, the lady put the handkerchief in her sleeve. It was a good thing I came. They all need me there. I'm their caretaker, sort of."

She was finished. There was silence in the room, and although she no longer spoke, she felt her voice lingering in the air. She opened her desk lid and rearranged the papers inside. Miss Hunter took a breath. "Roses in January, Maggie?" and finally everybody could laugh.

CHAPTER TWENTY-FIVE

❧

"I skipped school today," Maggie said. "I went out the front door, and then, when my aunts went into the parlor, I sneaked in the back door and I came up here." She looked at Timothy John and Miss Christabel and waited for their responses.

"Then you'll have to learn some lessons from *us*," Miss Christabel said. "Timothy John, what lessons do we know?"

Timothy John thought awhile. "Lessons," he said. "We used to know lessons, didn't we, Miss Christabel? I can't seem to remember them, though," and he consulted his scrap of newspaper. "How about washtubs?" he asked after a while.

"Washtubs aren't a proper school subject," Miss Christabel said. "She should be taught Latin. Or botany."

"Ah, yes, Latin," Timothy John answered. "Or botany.

Which one is botany—animals or rocks?"

"It's plants," Maggie told him.

"It's flowers," Miss Christabel said.

"Flowers!" Timothy John exclaimed. "Let's do that." He picked up Juniper in his basket and led the way into the garden. "Now," he said, when they had all arranged themselves in front of the roses on the wallpaper. "We will start with the blossom. Who knows what the blossom is? Juniper, do you?" But Juniper only growled in his basket. "Maggie?"

Maggie tried to remember what she had learned in science once about blossoms. Something about sepals and stamens and pistons. No, that was cars. Pistols. No. Something like that. "It's the flower part. With the petals, so you can tell if it's a rose. And it's where plants reproduce," she added, remembering something else.

"I don't think that's right," Miss Christabel said, and she bent her head close to a single rose on the wall. "It looks to me like a dancer in a Gypsy costume," she said. "Don't you think so, Timothy John? Look, these are her scarves. Crimson silk scarves. See how they float in the wind when she spins? I think the blossom must be a Gypsy dancer."

Timothy John bent over and examined the flower with her. "Yes, and this bud is the Gypsy baby. See? It's all swaddled in scraps and tatters. At any moment now it will kick its way out. Put your ear to the vine, Maggie, and see if you can hear it cry."

Maggie did as she was told, half expecting to hear a tiny whimper from the flowered paper, but there was no sound, and she pulled away. "I can't hear anything," she said.

"Then it must be asleep," Timothy John answered. "What about the leaves? Who knows what leaves are? Maggie?"

Maggie looked at the green leaves twining up and down the trellis in their steady rhythm: leaves, big rose; leaves, small rose; leaves, big rose; leaves, small rose. "I don't know," she said. "They store food or something." No, that wasn't right. What did leaves do?

Miss Christabel put her face up against the wall. "They're castanets," she said. "They're the Gypsy's castanets. Wait for the wind to blow, and you'll hear them shake. There! There they go! Listen, Maggie."

Maggie closed her eyes and imagined a faint clatter of slim wooden scoops shaking at her ear, but she tossed her head quickly and stared again at the design on the wallpaper. What kind of lesson was this, anyway?

"There now," Timothy John declared. "We have learned all about flowers today."

"You left out the thorns," Miss Christabel reminded him.

"The thorns!" Timothy John exclaimed, and he let his hand dart from spot to spot on the wallpaper. "Sharp, sharp, sharp," and he pulled his arm back rapidly. "Maggie, tell everybody what thorns are."

What were thorns? Those hidden arrows that made tiny

beads of blood spring out of your fingertips. "I don't know," she said.

"But you must know," Timothy John insisted. "Look at them again. What do they make you think of?"

Maggie leaned down to look at the thorns on the wall. What did they make her think of? The little black barbs on the paper were blunt and harmless, faded speckles among leaves and buds. Suddenly she had a thought. "They're hooks," she said, "for catching the Gypsy's scarves on, so they won't blow away."

Miss Christabel and Timothy John both stopped still. "That's wonderful!" Timothy John exclaimed. "What a wonderful answer! Hooks to catch scarves on! Miss Christabel, isn't that wonderful? Maggie taught something to *us* today. Maggie, that was truly wonderful."

Maggie thought about what she had said. It *was* nice. Like a poem; and she smiled a little.

There were shimmering ribbons of rain at the window, and only the palest of light settled on the little table. The two dolls held their hands above the kettle—"for warmth," they said—and their fingers now and then caught the faint glow of its copper dome. Maggie drew closer—it *did* seem warmer at the table—and looked across at the two doll faces, glowing, too, in the copper shine. She put her hand out to them for a quick moment.

"Please," she whispered. "Let me live here with you. All the time. We could have lessons and I could make your tea and water the roses. You could be my teachers and I could be your—your caretaker or something. We could *belong* to each other."

"But then you wouldn't be our visitor," Miss Christabel objected.

"I could be your all-the-time visitor," Maggie suggested.

"That's not a visitor," Miss Christabel answered. "That's a member of the household."

"I could be that, then. I could be the member of the household that takes care of you and fixes you when you break."

"That makes no sense at all," Timothy John said. "Who would come to visit?"

"But you didn't always have a visitor," Maggie said. "What did you use to do before I came?"

"Waited," said Miss Christabel.

"Waited for what?"

"For our visitor."

Maggie looked at them both. "For me, you mean? All you did was wait for me? But for how long?"

"Until you came," Timothy John replied.

"No, I mean how long have you been here? When did you first come? When did you first start waiting?"

"When did we first come?" Timothy John repeated, and he lifted his newspaper scrap to his face and studied it a long time. "Wednesday," he finally said.

"No, how many *years* ago?"

"How many years ago was Wednesday?" Timothy John asked Miss Christabel.

"A good many," she replied.

"A good many," he told Maggie. "Although there were many that were not good at all."

Maggie looked at the newspaper. "That's when you first came here?" she said. "When that newspaper is from? Eigh*teen* something? But that's maybe a hundred years ago. You've been here a hundred years?"

A hundred years. How many girls could have lived in the school downstairs all that time? A hundred? Two hundred? A thousand? All those girls, all those years, and not one knew that no more than a few dozen yards away a tiny household bustled, drank tea, watered roses, read, spoke, swept, petted a growling dog, listened maybe.

"Maybe I could be *both*," Maggie said suddenly. "Maybe I could be a member of the household *and* the visitor."

"Then you would be visiting yourself," Timothy John objected, "and that would make no sense. *You* are the visitor, *we* are the members of the household. One visitor. Two members of the household. Until the Other One comes, and then we will be three."

Maggie put her teacup down. "What other one? What do you mean? Who else is coming here?"

"There is one more of us to come," Miss Christabel said, holding the teapot over her cup, "and then we will be quite complete."

"Who?" Maggie demanded. "Who's coming? You mean another doll?"

"Another doll? But we have no dolls as it is."

"I mean, will it be as big as you or as big as me?"

"Neither," Timothy John answered. "It will be exactly as big as itself, from its feet to its head. Not one inch bigger."

"But how big?" Maggie persisted. "Will it fit on one of these chairs?"

"Sit," Timothy John corrected, "not fit. One sits on a chair."

"Will it sit on one of these chairs, then? Will it?"

"Of course it will sit on one," Miss Christabel said. "There's no need to sit on two."

It was a doll, then. "But when is it going to come?"

"When?" Miss Christabel carried the sugar spoon back and forth between the little bowl and her cup. "When it is time. Come, finish your tea. Look, Timothy John. The vapors have begun to curl her hair, just as we said they would."

"That's quite right," Timothy John agreed. "You have changed, Maggie."

"Me?" Maggie looked down at her feet. "How have I changed?"

[212]

"The roses have changed you," Miss Christabel said. "Their glow has come off on your face, as we said. And the bread has fattened your wrists."

"Look in the mirror," Timothy John said, "and see for yourself."

The mirror hung like a picture above her bedroom sink, holding within its frame a piece of gray sky, a rain-dark branch, and an expanse of plaster wall. Maggie put herself in the scene. It was true: Her face *was* fuller. The shadow that used to fall just below her cheekbone was gone, and her chin had lost its sharp point. Her hair, too, no longer lay like wet weeds against her neck, but fluffed out around her ears. Was it really because of the roses and the wooden slabs of bread and the empty cups of tea?

She seized her brush and, tilting her head to the side so that her hair fell on one shoulder, began striking at it with the sharp bristles until it floated out like a chiffon scarf around her face. Nice. She looked nice in the mirror. She had hardly looked in the mirror since she had shown off its powers to the Backwoods Girls.

The Backwoods Girls. How long had it been since she had last called them to her and guided them through the many wonders of her room? It was hard to remember. A month, maybe. Two. She looked now at these same wonders—the pen on the desk, the playing cards (when had she last played solitaire?), the chest of drawers—and she felt no urge to show them off to anyone.

"Maggie!" It was Aunt Lillian. Maggie watched the color drain from the face in the mirror as she remembered suddenly that she had skipped school that day and had forgotten to come back through the front door at three o'clock.

"Maggie!" Aunt Lillian's voice came from the garden, and Maggie went to the window. It was still raining, and two black umbrellas, like a pair of giant toadstools suddenly sprung from the earth, moved to the birch trees, to the rose beds, back to the birches.

"Maggie!" the aunts called, first one and then the other. "Maggie!"

She retreated from the window and stood against the wall. Presently a door slammed and Aunt Lillian called from somewhere below. "Maggie!"

She stepped quietly into the corridor. "She's never skipped school before," she heard.

"Maybe she's run away."

"Children don't run away from homes where they are properly nourished."

"Then where can she have gone?"

"To see a friend."

"She has no friend."

There was a long silence. Then: "She was just beginning

to improve. She stopped sucking her hair. Have you noticed that?"

"It's her nutrition. Children with adequate nutrition have no need to suck their hair."

"And her face. It's beginning to fill out."

It was true, then. Even her aunts had noticed.

"Maybe something happened on the way to school."

"Not likely. She would have been seen."

There was a new tone in their voices now. Worry. They were worried about her. They noticed that her face looked fuller and her hair wasn't wet anymore, and they were worried that something had happened to her—that she had been hurt. Killed, even. Maybe they thought she had been struck by a car or something.

"Maggie!" The voices were closer now. *"Maggie!"*

"What?" she answered from the upstairs hall.

In a moment both aunts were at the bottom of the stairs. "How did you get up there?" one cried, and then the other: "Where have you been?"

She walked down one step at a time while the two aunts called out repeatedly, "Where were you?" from below. It didn't matter what they said. They were relieved to see her. Her face was fuller and they were happy that she hadn't been killed.

"Into the parlor," Aunt Harriet commanded when she reached the bottom step. Both aunts seated themselves side by side on the sofa before they uttered another word, their gray hair and gray clothes fading into the gray of the cushions. "Sit down," Aunt Lillian ordered.

"Why weren't you in school today?" Aunt Harriet demanded. How did they know, come to think of it, that she had skipped school?

"I got sick," she answered.

"Sick? The nurse didn't say you were sick. She said you hadn't been to school at all." That was how. The nurse.

"I mean I got sick on the way and I came back. And I didn't want to bother you, so I stayed outside. In the fresh air." That was good. They liked fresh air. Anyway, it didn't matter what she said. They were glad she was alive.

"It's been raining all day," Aunt Lillian said.

That was true. Little moist points were attacking the parlor windows even now. Why had she said that?

"You are keeping something from us."

"You are a sneak."

"You are a truant."

"You were hiding somewhere."

"Where do you hide?"

"What do you do?"

"Where do you go?"

Maggie allowed her eyes to travel around the room like a slow train on a track, stopping here, starting up, stopping there. The man in the portrait gazed at her steadily from under his reddish hair. The woman in the next frame wore a handkerchief tucked into her sleeve. Did everybody do that in those days? A gray curtain, like an oblong of rain itself, hung at each rainy window. The ivory elephants marched in their silent parade, little ones first, big ones at the end, on the shelf of the curio cabinet. The china ballerina balanced on the tip of her shiny toe.

"Where do you go?"

"What do you do?"

"Answer!"

But Maggie didn't answer. Something had caught her eye. How was it she had never noticed it before? She inched her chair sideways across the rug to get a better view, and lowered her head to her shoulder.

"Sit up straight or you will damage your spine."

Behind the curio cabinet, at eye level now, a slender clasp had been driven into the wall, and from it, like a mouse in the grip of a claw, hung a small black key.

CHAPTER TWENTY-SIX

❧❧

Margaret Ann Turner
Grade 6, Room 8
April 19

The Rose

The rose is a plant that grows on a vine.

It consists of blossoms, buds, leaves, roots, and thorns.

The blossom part is a Gypsy dancer that throws its red silk scarves in the air.

The bud is the Gypsy baby that's all wrapped up tight in little scraps. Pretty soon it will kick its way out and wave its scarves around too. Sometimes you can hear it cry.

The leaves are the Gypsy's castanets that shake in the wind.

The rose swallows water through its roots, which are the throat of the plant.

The best part is the thorns. The thorns are for catching the silk scarves on so they won't blow away.

Maggie stared at the report as it lay inside her desk. A scattering of small red question marks dotted the page like a shower of tiny sea horses, and a red U, neat and stiff, stood at the bottom like a toy pail ready to receive them. U. In her old school, and the one before that, U stood for Unsatisfactory. Here it meant Unacceptable, but it was still the lowest grade you could get. "You didn't follow the proper procedure for writing a nature report," Miss Hunter had written across the top. "What are your references? Where is your bibliography? *SEE ME!*"

Maggie's desk lid lay partially open, and under it she worked a pair of scissors around and around a scrap of lace she had found at the bottom of the remnant box in the classroom cupboard; she let the loose threads fall across her report on the rose. The lace had come from the border of a window curtain, maybe, or an old petticoat. It was woven with little lilies of the valley and tiny rosebuds, and it was exactly right for a shawl for Miss Christabel to wear to the party.

The party had been Maggie's idea. "Don't you ever do

anything special around here?" she had asked the dolls once. "I mean, don't you ever have Thanksgiving or Christmas or anything? Don't you have birthdays?"

"Birthdays?" Timothy John had replied. "But we wouldn't know when they were. We don't have years, you know. There's no way of telling when they've gone by."

Maggie had thought about that then. Without a calendar, without any contact with the world outside, how would they know when a holiday came or went? "You can't have years," Timothy John had gone on, "unless you have things that change with them. Flowers that bloom and die and bloom again, and animals that grow longer in the leg."

It was true: Nothing changed in the attic; the roses clung in eternal bloom to their paper vine, Juniper remained forever the size of Maggie's thumb, the news in Timothy John's paper told of the same fiery event, and the world outside the window could be viewed only with the aid of a chair.

"We could *make* a special day," Maggie had said, "and I could tell you when it came each year. We could have a party, and it could be like our own special day that nobody would know about." What day? It had been March then; all the holidays had gone by. Her own birthday had gone by. Along with two other girls whose birthdays fell in the same month, she had been given a calendar in school one day at lunchtime, and there had been cupcakes with candles for dessert, instead of stewed fruit.

"We could celebrate the day you first came here," she had suggested. "May fourteenth. It could be like your birthday. For both of you. Or an anniversary. And for Juniper, too. We could have a party with presents and I could bring cake and we could put ribbons around the table." Maggie had never been to a real birthday party, and she made up what she could from remembering scenes in books. "We could have it every year. Could we do that?"

Timothy John and Miss Christabel had cocked their heads toward each other and remained that way for a long time. "But birthdays are what make people grow older," Timothy John said. "If we have birthdays, we'll get wrinkles."

"You already have wrinkles," Miss Christabel answered. "Especially in your jacket."

"You'll only get older once a year," Maggie told them.

"That's true," Timothy John said. "The rest of the time we'll stay the same."

"A party!" Miss Christabel exclaimed. "We'll have to shine the kettle."

Maggie moved her scissors in and out along the edges of the lace, folding and smoothing until it was just the right shape, narrow at the top, wide at the bottom.

In the front of the room, Miss Hunter was filling the blackboard with long-division brackets. Houses, she called them. "The dividend is *inside* the house, under the roof," she was saying. "The quotient is on top of the roof, and the divisor waits at the door."

Maggie lifted her eyes from the lace and looked around at her classmates. Carolyn was extracting a thick wad of paper strips from the tunnel of her spiral notebook. Alyssa had drawn a large A on the edge of her sneaker sole and was now inking it in with stripes and circles. Gregory was crushing the point of his pencil between the teeth of his loose-leaf rings. Sharon was peeling a continuous snake of paper from her crayon. Maggie held the piece of lace up in front of her eyes and peered through its spidery threads. Everything in the room suddenly took on a network of cracks as she moved her head behind the lace—the floor, the windows, the walls, and each of the faces around her.

She returned the little shawl to the well of her desk and smoothed it out, tracing with her fingernail the frail network of blossom and leaf, imagining Miss Christabel's face surrounded by its folds. They would all be in the garden the day of the party—Miss Christabel against the wallpaper roses and Timothy John at her side. He would be wearing a new ribbon around his neck, one that Maggie was going to make from a fringe of the drapery in the parlor, and he would be holding Juniper. There would be something new for Juniper, too, but she hadn't decided what. Best of all would be the present she was saving as a surprise—it would be back in the little room, and it was the most wonderful present ever.

"What a lovely shawl," Miss Christabel would say, and she would draw the lace close around her shoulders.

"Yes, and here's something else," Maggie would answer. "A gold clasp to keep it from sliding off your shoulders," and she would fasten the shawl with a little brass tack she had just discovered in the corner of her desk. "It's all gold," and right now she slipped its slender wings between two openings in the lace design and held it up again to see how it looked in the light.

Suddenly she sensed a change in the room, and in another moment she noticed the stillness. Miss Hunter was still, the chalk was still, the pens and pencils and crayons were still. Nothing stirred. Maggie lowered her desk lid and looked around. Everything was like a photograph. Miss Hunter stood frozen in front of the room, her eyes fixed on Maggie. All the other faces, shattered only a moment before into tangles of lacy cracks, were now smooth and whole and turned, too, toward Maggie. Hurriedly she returned the scrap of cloth to her desk and folded her hands on its lid, keeping her eyes fastened all the while on the blackboard with its powdery patterns of brackets and numbers.

"Well?" Miss Hunter seemed to be waiting for an answer. Maggie looked up at her. An answer to what? "Where is your work?" Miss Hunter was moving down the aisle now. What work? For a minute Maggie thought she was referring to the lace. She looked around. A notebook lay on every desk but hers. Apparently math was over and they had moved on to something else. She opened her desk lid to extract her own notebook, but a hand shot in ahead of hers, and in the next moment Miss Hunter was crushing Miss Christabel's shawl into a tight wad and marching with it to the corner of the room, where she held it above the wastebasket and finally let it drop upon a bed of silvery pencil shavings and chalk stubs.

"Here, I got this for you." It was the end of the day, and they were getting their coats from the hooks in the corridor. Barbara was standing next to her, holding something in her hand. "What's it for, anyway?" Maggie looked into Barbara's open palm and saw the little scrap of lace, crumpled now, like a used paper doily, and smudged here and there with gray. Maggie put her arms into the sleeves of her coat and began to button it up. "It's nothing," she said. "I don't want it. It's just an old piece of rag."

Barbara examined it. "Can I have it?"

"Yeah, sure. I don't care. It's just an old rag."

"What were you doing with it, then?"

"Nothing. Just messing."

"But I saw you cutting it out. Like you were making something. What were you making?"

Maggie finally looked up at Barbara's face. There was no mockery there; nothing, in fact, but curiosity. "What were you making?" Barbara repeated.

Everyone else from the class had moved down the hall, and Barbara and Maggie were alone in front of the coat hooks. "A shawl," Maggie finally said.

"A shawl? Who for?"

"For this lady I know."

"You mean the lady that you told about at Sharing? With the roses and all?"

"Yeah, her."

"Then how come it's so small?"

Maggie looked back at Miss Christabel's lace lying twisted in Barbara's palm, and she suddenly wanted it back. "I mean, it's for her doll," she said, and her hand darted out like a diving bird, snatching the scrap of cloth away. She stuffed it into her pocket and began edging down the hall to keep Barbara from grabbing it back again.

"Oh, is it a costume doll?" Barbara asked, following her.

"Yeah. No. I don't know. Sort of. Yeah."

They were side by side now, walking down the stairs together, and Maggie tried to see herself through someone else's eyes: Maggie and another girl walking downstairs together, talking, like other people, like friends.

"What country?"

"What *country*?"

"Yeah, is it from Holland or Poland or what?"

"Is what from Holland?"

"The *cos*tume doll."

"Oh." Maggie thought. "It's from around here."

"Then what's so special about it?"

What was so special about Miss Christabel? Miss *Chris*tabel? She was her*self*, that's what. She was *real*. She and Timothy John lived in this wonderful place in the attic that nobody else in the whole world knew about—a wonderful place where it was warm and happy and they . . . what? They liked her a whole lot. And she liked them. Loved.

"So what's so special about it?" Barbara asked again.

"Nothing. She has these old-fashioned clothes."

"Can I see her?"

Could she see her? See Miss Christabel? See Timothy John and Juniper? What would that be like? Maggie wondered. "These are the dolls," she would say, leading Barbara into the hidden room in the attic. "This one's name is Miss Christabel and this one's name is Timothy John and this is supposed to be their dog. His name is Juniper." And Barbara would say, "Ooh, can we dress them in different clothes?" and then all of a sudden Miss Christabel would rise from the table and start bringing in extra dishes from the china cupboard, while Timothy John would read aloud from his newspaper and Juniper would growl from under the table.

"Can I see it or not?" Barbara asked.

"No. It's this lady's. She doesn't let anyone touch it except me." Everything she said made less sense than before.

"Not even to look at?"

"No."

They were down at the front door by now. "I have some costume dolls you can look at," Barbara said. "You want to see them sometime at my house?"

Maggie looked up. No one had ever invited her to visit before. No one. Ever. "I don't know," she said. "Maybe."

❦

"Could I bring somebody here?" Maggie asked. "For a visit, sort of?"

"Somebody here?" Both dolls rose together.

"Mercy!" Miss Christabel cried.

"But you must never do that!" Timothy John said.

"Why not?"

"We must never be seen," Timothy John answered, and his china hands clicked together.

"But you've been seen by *me.*"

"That's different. You are the right one."

"But suppose someone else saw you?" Maggie asked. "What would happen?"

"That would be quite dreadful," he answered. "If we were seen, we would—"

"Timothy John!" Miss Christabel interrupted. "No one must see us," she said, turning to Maggie, and both dolls fell silent.

"Look," Maggie said after a long while, "I've brought you something for the party," and she unfolded the little lace shawl. "Mercy!" Miss Christabel cried. "A new table-cloth. How lovely. Look, Timothy John. A new cloth for the table."

"It's a shawl," Maggie corrected.

"A new shawl for the table," Miss Christabel said. "To keep its shoulders warm. What a fine idea. Let's see if it fits."

"No, it's for you, Miss Christabel," Maggie said, "to keep *your* shoulders warm," and she gathered the lace around Miss Christabel's neck and secured it with the brass tack. "It's to wear to the party."

Miss Christabel turned her head first to one shoulder and then to the other. "A shawl," she said. "How very splendid."

"With a little golden moon," Timothy John added, fingering the brass tack, "to light up your chin, in case you can't find it in the dark."

"I've brought something for you, too, Timothy John,"

Maggie said, and she handed him the braided drapery fringe.

"Look, Miss Christabel!" he exclaimed. "Maggie has gotten me a new bellpull. What a useful thing to have. I can hang it on the wall and call you when you are in the garden."

"But we have no bell," Miss Christabel pointed out.

"That's what's so wonderful about it," Timothy John answered. "It's a silent bellpull. For use at night, when you don't want to wake anyone up. Thank you, Maggie. It's an admirable bellpull."

"It's a necktie," Maggie said. "With a tie clasp to hold it together. See? Here's how it works," and she tied the braided fringe around his neck, connecting the ends with a paper clip. Timothy John tucked his chin in to look more closely. "Lovely," he said. "Quite lovely. A bellpull you wear around your neck, so you don't have to get up to ring it."

"It will go with your Sunday clothes," Miss Christabel commented.

"Sunday clothes?" Maggie asked. "What Sunday clothes?"

"We both have Sunday clothes," Timothy John replied. "But we haven't worn them yet, because it never gets to be Sunday. It's always Wednesday."

"Where are they?" Maggie asked. "What are they like?"

"Let's get them out, Timothy John, and see how they look. They're in the chest, under the paper."

Timothy John and Miss Christabel bent over the clothes

chest, and together they lifted out small squares of linen until they reached a single layer of thin paper, stiff and crackly. "Ah, there it is," Miss Christabel said, peeling the paper back and bringing forth a wrinkled black dress. "My best silk." She held it up to her shoulders. Its long sleeves ended in white pleated cuffs, and a row of tiny buttons, starting at the collar, proceeded down the front to the hem. It was like the dresses everybody wore long ago, like the dress on the woman in the portrait, like the dresses in old-fashioned books, and it rustled when it shook.

"But what happened to the bottom?" Maggie noticed. "It's all ragged. It's been *burned!*"

"No," Miss Christabel replied. "The part that's *gone* has been burned. The part that's here is perfectly good."

"But how did it get burned?"

"It isn't burned," Miss Christabel responded. "I just explained that. Do you think it still fits, Timothy John?" She kicked out first one foot and then the other behind its skirt.

But Timothy John was busily removing a black wool suit from beneath the paper, and he didn't answer. "Here's the waistcoat," he said instead, unfolding a sleeveless garment with smooth white buttons. "And look!" he cried, slipping his hand into a slim pocket. "My gold watch! It's still here!" He held a tiny gold disk on a chain and listened to it against his ear. "And it still says the right time. Eight thirty-five."

"That's not the right time," Maggie said. "It's only about four o'clock."

"No," Timothy John answered, showing her the face. "It says eight thirty-five. The time we arrived. And look, Miss Christabel. Here are the pants. Beautiful as ever."

"But they're burned, too!" Maggie exclaimed, examining the cuffs. "How did they get burned?"

"Listen, Timothy John," Miss Christabel interrupted, and she shook her silk dress in the air. "It still rustles. Do you remember how I used to rustle in my Sunday dress when I walked down the stairs?"

Maggie looked from one doll to the other. Down what stairs? "You mean you used to go downstairs?" she asked. "To the rest of the house?" A picture came to her now of Miss Christabel bumping down the center stairs of the big house below and rustling through its rooms; climbing onto one of the chairs in the dining room, her head coming just to the edge of the table; standing at the open door of the refrigerator, no taller than its bottom shelf; settling in a corner of the gray sofa, her legs stuck out straight before her, stiff in their little boots. "Down what stairs?" Maggie asked, but neither doll answered.

"And what will *you* wear, Maggie?" Timothy John asked instead. "What are *your* Sunday clothes?"

What would she wear? "I don't know," she answered.

There was nothing in her closet but the clothes she wore to school. "Maybe something nice in my hair. A flower or something. There are some flowers in the garden now. I could wear one of those."

"That would be nice," Timothy John said. "Roses would look just right in your hair. Let's pick one out now."

"No, I don't mean this garden. I mean the outside one. Downstairs."

"Ah, downstairs," Timothy John sighed, and Maggie wondered if he, too, had wandered up and down the long corridors, looking in bedroom doors, the top of his hat no higher than a wastebasket. "What about downstairs?" she asked, but "Downstairs roses die" was all he answered.

The party was less than three weeks away. Everything was ready—or almost ready. The ribbon streamers were all laid out—Maggie had cut one of Aunt Harriet's silk scarves into slender strips of shimmery red—and the cupcakes would come from next week's birthday lunch at school. The big present— the wonderful one, the surprise for Miss Christabel and Timothy John—was still to be gotten, but Juniper's gift, wrapped in a crayoned napkin, already lay alongside the little black key in her dresser drawer. She had gotten it just two days earlier—from Barbara.

"Guess which hand," Barbara had said, coming up to Maggie in the school yard with her fists stretched in front of her. Maggie had been standing alone near the fence, her back to the recess games.

"What?" she asked.

"Guess which *hand*," Barbara had repeated, bringing her hands closer to Maggie's stomach.

"Which hand what?"

"Which hand has the *surprise*, dummy. Pick a hand."

Maggie contemplated the two rows of shiny knuckles. "This one," she finally said, pointing to Barbara's left hand and then stepping back quickly as if it might explode.

"Wrong," Barbara said, opening her fingers and displaying an empty palm. She put both hands behind her back. "Try again," and she thrust her fists forward once more.

"This one."

"Wrong again," and Barbara shuffled her hands behind her. "Now try."

"This one." Maggie touched the same hand. It was probably a dumb trick. There really wasn't any surprise at all, and Barbara would continue to expose one empty hand after another.

"Right," and Barbara unfolded her fingers one at a time, revealing a furled paper parasol, purple and red, across her palm.

Maggie leaned over to look at it. "What is it?"

"What *is* it? What do you *think* it is? It's a *parasol*. My mother got it at this restaurant she went to. It's for you. I don't need it. I already have a million of them."

Maggie watched as Barbara spread open its toothpick ribs, and the thin paper unfolded like a butterfly wing. "You can hook it so it stays open," Barbara said, showing her the little latch that held the paper circle open. "Watch it spin," and the purple and red flowers melted into a twirling magenta wheel as she twisted the handle against her thumb.

"It's nice," Maggie said, looking at it. It *was* nice. It could be for Juniper, she thought. She could prop it up in the patch of sunlight on the floor in the attic garden, and he could lie under it in his basket while Miss Christabel and Timothy John strolled among the wicker chairs and paper roses. "It's just right," she said, and at last she received it into her own hand. "The colors and everything." She, too, spun it, holding it to the sun and letting the light stain her fingers red, purple, red again.

"Just right for what?" Barbara asked. "What are you going to do with it?"

"I don't know. Take it to this party I'm going to."

"You're going to a party?" Barbara looked up at her. "Whose? Is it someone from this class?"

"No."

"Then who?"

"Nobody you know."

"Then what's the parasol for?"

"I don't know. It could be for a present or something."

"But it only costs about a penny. They give them away free at this restaurant my mother goes to. Who would want a present like that?"

"We have brought you something to wear to the party," Aunt Harriet said. Maggie hurriedly slammed the drawer containing Juniper's present, the little cupcake and candle, and the slender black key, and spun around to the two aunts standing in the doorway of her room, a large flat box between them.

What party?

"Wash your hands before trying it on," Aunt Harriet said, advancing into the room and laying the box on the bed. "And don't hunch your shoulders. Poor posture ruins fine clothing."

What clothing? What party? Maggie pressed her back to the dresser drawer. "What party?" she asked, her voice a croak.

"The party on the fourteenth. Stop working your teeth like that. You'll get gumboils."

The party on the fourteenth? The *dolls'* party? How had they found out? "How do you know about the party?"

"We have bought you an expensive dress," Aunt Harriet was saying, "and we expect your conduct to do it justice." She picked at the twine around the box. "Pretty dresses do nothing to conceal disgraceful behavior."

"Wash your hands," Aunt Lillian said. "And your face, too. There's something nasty on your cheek."

The next moment Aunt Harriet was lifting a dress from a snowbank of tissue paper, and Maggie caught her breath. Was this really for her? She had never seen anything so beautiful, and for a moment she forgot to wonder how her aunts had found out about the party in the attic. The dress was printed with tiny violets, a frill of cream lace trimmed the collar and the bottom of each sleeve, and a purple velvet ribbon hung from tiny loops at either side of the waist. Maggie took it from her aunt's hand and held it up to her shoulders, as Miss Christabel had done with her own best dress, leaning down to see if the hem fell to the right distance from the floor, and reaching out against the skirt first with one foot and then the other.

The next instant her hands were pulled above her head, and the dress, the wonderful dress, was lowered over her shoulders.

"It sags at the waist," Aunt Lillian said, standing back and putting her head to one side.

"The shoulders droop," Aunt Harriet said.

"The skirt is too long."

Maggie looked up at them in alarm, wondering if they would take the dress away from her.

"It will have to do," Aunt Lillian said. "There's no time to find another."

"The sleeves are too long," Aunt Harriet said. "The lace will get into the tea when she serves."

Maggie stepped back against the dresser drawer again. How did they know about the party? How did they know about the tea? Had they found the cupcake and candle? Had they opened her drawer and seen the napkin with the parasol? Her heart stopped. Had they seen the key? *"What tea?"* she shouted. *"What party?"*

Both aunts froze in front of her. "Stop that shouting. If you're going to engage in improper behavior, you will be unfit to present to the members of the society, and there will *be* no party."

What were they talking about? "What society?"

"The Health Society," Aunt Harriet said. "You've been told about that." She spoke as though Maggie were deaf and could only read lips.

Oh, that. "That's on the fourteenth? That meeting?"

"It's not a meeting. It's the society's annual party. And we're presenting you as an example of how good nutrition improves one's physical appearance."

"And behavior," Aunt Lillian put in.

Maggie stared at them some more. That's what this dress was for? The Health Society meeting?

"There are socks, too," Aunt Lillian said, and she drew out a pair of white knee socks, smooth and flat and curved perfectly at the calf. "But we can't go ahead with our plans if you are going to disgrace us with infantile behavior."

"I thought you had outgrown your tantrums," Aunt Harriet said.

"And your impudence," Aunt Lillian added.

They were at the door now. "Hang the dress on a hanger, and don't handle it with unwashed hands. And fold the socks neatly. Wrinkled socks are unsightly."

Maggie stood on the bed after they had left and stretched herself tall so she could see in the mirror to the bottom of the new dress. The hem fell too far below her knee, and the belt line hung loose on her waist, but she tightened the velvet ribbon, the wonderful velvet ribbon that rippled into pale streams when you drew your fingernail across its nap and felt like cat's ear against your lips. She stepped down to the floor and opened the dresser drawer, looking in at the party things. Aunt Harriet and Aunt Lillian hadn't found her out, after all. The cupcake and candle were safe, Juniper's present was safe, the little black key was safe, and she had a Sunday-best dress of her own to wear to the dolls' party in the attic.

CHAPTER TWENTY-EIGHT

❦

She should have brought a pair of scissors. The lilac stem didn't snap in two as she had supposed; it merely bent like a reed, and in the end she had to tear it from the shrub with her teeth. The aroma penetrated her nose and settled now in her throat—an aching, beautiful lavender taste. She held the blossom in her hand, as lightly as though it were an injured bird, and brushed with a careful finger its quivering plumage. So very small the flowers were, each containing deep in its pit what she had never noticed before—a pinch of yellow talc. In a little while, after putting on her new dress, she would attach the stem to her hair and face herself in the mirror. She would look pretty, she knew, and she held the blossom against her hair now to see how it felt.

There was a rustle from somewhere at her back, and she spun around, putting the flower behind her. A black sphere moved slowly among the branches of a clump of trees across the lawn, and a moment later she made out the form of Uncle Morris under his bowler, with the head of his walking stick flitting before him like a giant silver bee.

"Lovely," he said, brushing the crown of his hat against his sleeve.

She brought the lilac forward. He had seen it in her hair. He had seen her looking pretty. "It is precisely right," he continued, and she felt the corners of her lips twitch into a momentary smile. "They will like it," he added.

Her hand dropped. "Who will? Who will like it?"

"They will. The two of them."

Maggie's breath caught in her chest. What did he know? "The two of who?"

"The two of your *ears*," Uncle Morris replied, restoring the hat to his head. "You do have two, don't you? Ah, yes, there they are. How clever of you to wear one on each side of your head, so that you can be picked up like a vase, if necessary, and placed somewhere else."

Maggie let out her breath.

"Here," he said, taking the lilac from her hand and tucking it behind her left ear. "Lilacs are their favorite flower, you know, next to roses," and once more Maggie held her breath. *Whose* favorite flower? "But you'll need two," he continued, "one for each," and he twisted a second sprig from the lilac bush.

Maggie stared at him. "Each of who?" she whispered.

"Each of your *ears*." He held out the blossom, and her hand reached out for an instant. "You will want to look your best today," he went on. "This is an important day for all of you," and Maggie stepped back, not taking the flower. "For all of who?"

"For all of *you*: your head, your knees, your thumbs, your anklebones. But mostly your ears."

Maggie looked at him a long time and then turned toward the house, feeling his gaze on her back like a warming hand. Once, thinking he was following, she looked around, but he was standing where she had left him, staring fixedly at her and twirling the lilac between his fingers like a paper parasol.

"There you are, Maggie. I've been calling you." It was Aunt Harriet's voice she heard, but the dining room was empty. It smelled of furniture polish, sharp and lemony, and Maggie shielded the lilac with her hand, keeping its own smell to itself. "We'll need help carrying in the tea things," the voice went on, and Maggie at last spotted her aunt under the dining table, rubbing its massive claw with an orange-streaked rag. "The raw cauliflower will go at one end of the table and the celery hearts at the other. The cookies and tea things will go in the center. What is that I smell?" she demanded, backing out along the floor. "Are you wearing perfume?"

"No, it's this flower," Maggie answered. "I'm going to wear it today. It matches my dress."

"You've been in the garden, then. Wash your hands before handling the tableware. And put the flower outside. It has mealybugs. What's that in your other hand?"

"Nothing. It's for my hair." Maggie pressed the little black key into her palm and covered it with her thumb.

"Where are you hurrying off to?"

"Nowhere. Into the parlor."

"Don't touch anything."

"No."

Aunt Lillian was clearing away the coats from the clothes rack in the front hall. "What were you doing in the parlor?" she demanded.

"Nothing," Maggie answered. "Polishing furniture."

"I hope you didn't disturb anything."

"No."

"Straighten your shoulders when you walk. What's that in your hair?"

"It's a flower. To go with my dress."

"Throw it out. It has aphids. What do you have behind your back?"

"Nothing. It's just this rag. For polishing the furniture."
Maggie had reached the stairs by now, and she mounted
them quickly, the orange-streaked rag, heavy with its prize,
clasped against her stomach.

"We will expect you to be dressed and clean by two-thirty,"
her aunt called after her. "Make sure the wax is cleaned
from your ears, and wash your hands and face. And arms. I
don't want to see rivers on your arms. And throw away that
rag. It will stain your dress."

Maggie was at the top of the stairs now, and Aunt Lillian's
voice followed her to her room. "Make sure you speak in
a clear voice when people address you. And keep your knees
together when you sit."

Maggie was all dressed, as she had been asked, at two-
thirty. Her socks were pulled up so that the ribs were perfectly
straight and the folded cuffs exactly even. The two ends of
the velvet ribbon on her dress were exactly even, too, and
the loops of the bow lay flat and horizontal against her back,
not upright as her bows usually turned out. She stood in
the center of her room and set herself into a rapid spin.
The skirt of her dress billowed out like a parachute, like a
bluebell, like the little paper parasol she was about to give
to Juniper, and the air rushing around her bare thighs felt
cool and good. She smoothed out her hair at the mirror and
secured the stem of the lilac blossom with a bobby pin.

She had never seen herself look so nice. "Isn't she pretty?" someone in her head said. "Lovely," someone else answered. "Lavender is just her color."

"Maggie!" Aunt Harriet's voice sailed up the stairs. "It's time you were down here."

Maggie opened the dresser drawer and removed the cupcake, the candle, the three matches she had taken earlier from the kitchen, and Juniper's present wrapped in a napkin.

"Maggie?"

There was no time to wrap the dolls' present in a napkin as well, and so she would give it to them in the dustrag with its streaks of furniture polish. It didn't matter. It was a wonderful present, and they wouldn't care how it was wrapped.

"Maggie?"

She opened the door and stepped out. "I'm coming," she answered as she made her way across the hall, her arms full. If she twisted her hips as she walked, her skirt would swish against her knees like petals in the wind, like Gypsy scarves.

"Check your nails," Aunt Lillian called up to her. "And make sure your nasal passages are clear. Maggie? Do you hear me?"

"Yes," and she continued along the hall, letting the ribbed cuffs of her socks rub rhythmically against each other.

"Did you do the back of your neck?" It was Aunt Harriet this time.

"Yes."

"What's taking you so long?" Aunt Lillian.

"Maggie?" Aunt Harriet. "They'll be here any minute."
And it was true: The moment Maggie turned the handle of
the door to the attic stairs she heard from the floor below
the distant, hollow gong, like the echo of a sigh, of the front
doorbell, and she knew the first guests had arrived.

"First come the presents," Maggie said, kneeling on the
attic floor. Miss Christabel wore her lace shawl over the black
silk dress with the long row of buttons, and Timothy John's
new tie was knotted at his chin. The room itself was hung
here and there with the ribbons cut from her aunt's scarf.
The table was decorated with more ribbons and laid with
the nicest dishes from the cabinet. It's going to be a good
party, Maggie thought, looking around, and she laid the two
packages on the floor—one wrapped in a paper napkin, the
other in an orange-stained rag.

"First yours, Juniper," she said. "Here, I'll help you unwrap
it. Look how nice it is!" She had never given anyone a real
present before, and she felt her voice quiver with excitement.
"It's a sunshade," she explained, "for lying under, so the
sun won't get in your eyes. Here, let me show you how it
works." She fastened the little latch and held it up to the
attic window. "Look what it does when it spins," she said.

[246]

"And it makes this nice pink shadow when you put it down. Do you like it? We can take it to the garden after the party, and you can lie under it and go to sleep."

Juniper growled very softly as Maggie placed him under the sunshade. The light filtered through the flowered paper, casting a pink glow on his head, and Maggie ran a finger along his cool china back. She felt good. It was a nice present. "It's yours to keep for always," she said. "It's something to remember me by," she added, recalling something that people in books said when they gave presents, and Juniper growled again.

"I wonder if it will turn his dreams pink," Miss Christabel remarked.

"And now I have a present for you, too," Maggie said, turning to Miss Christabel and Timothy John, and she led them over to the table. "It's for both of you together, and it's something you'll like a whole lot." She lifted the orange-stained package up to the table.

"I know what it is already," Timothy John said. "It's another headache cloth. With liniment on it."

"No, that's just the rag to cover it with," Maggie said. "And anyway, it's furniture polish. Look what's inside." Very gently, using the tips of two fingers from each hand, she lifted the cloth away.

At first Miss Christabel made a little gasping noise from

somewhere inside her head, and Timothy John's hands flew up to his face, but after that they were silent a long time as they gazed down at the table.

"I knew you would like it," Maggie said. "I knew it."

Finally Miss Christabel spoke in a whisper. "Selena," she said. "That's what we used to call her. Remember, Timothy John?"

"Selena," Timothy John repeated, whispering also. "She's still wearing the same skirt, and doing the same step. On one toe," and he reached out to touch with the fingers of his own china hand the china hand of the ballerina balancing on the table.

CHAPTER TWENTY-NINE

❧

"Remember when we first found her?" Miss Christabel asked. "Remember that day, Timothy John?"

They *had* been downstairs, then. "Found her where?" Maggie asked. "Remember what day? What are you talking about? How do you know about the ballerina?"

But neither doll answered. "How nice that she came back," Timothy John said.

"She didn't come back," Maggie said, raising her voice. "I gave her to you. She's a present. I got her. She was mine, sort of, and I gave her to you as a present." The surfaces of her eyes began to sting. "It was supposed to be a surprise," she added, her voice catching.

"It was," Timothy John said.

"I never thought we'd see her again," Miss Christabel put in. "Selena." And she leaned toward the figurine until their foreheads met with a little click.

"Again?" Maggie demanded. "What do you mean, *again?* When did you see her before?" Once more the dolls remained silent. *"When?"* Maggie repeated.

"Look," Timothy John said. "If we stand her next to the sugar bowl, she can lean on its edge when she grows tired."

"She might tip it over," Miss Christabel objected.

"Not if it is weighted down with sugar, which it always is," Timothy John assured her.

"When?" Maggie asked again.

"Timothy John," Miss Christabel said, "we must give Maggie *her* present now," and in a minute she returned from the clothes chest with a small package wrapped in the same yellowed paper that had covered the dolls' best clothing. "Happy Anniversary," she said, handing it over. "Happy Anniversary," Timothy John repeated, and both dolls drew closer as Maggie began to unfold the paper.

"Oh," she said at last. "A handkerchief of my very own," and she spread the tiny square cloth on her knee and looked at it a long time, smoothing it out now and then with the edge of her hand. Somehow the design looked familiar—roses and stems weaving in and out, in and out; she had seen that somewhere, on the border of a page or the edge of a gown. Where? "I've never had a real handkerchief before," she said. "Just the paper kind you blow your nose in and throw away." She couldn't remember when anyone had given *her* a real present before. "It's beautiful," she said, and she slipped it under the elastic of her cuff. "Look, Miss Christabel, now I'm just like you," and she held her arm next to the flowered handkerchief in the doll's sleeve.

"Just," Miss Christabel agreed.

"But we must get on with the party," Timothy John said, and he removed the little gold watch from his waistcoat pocket. "It's growing late," he said. "Eight thirty-five. At night. The last time I looked, it was eight thirty-five in the morning."

"It's neither," Maggie said. "That watch always says eight thirty-five."

"That explains why it's always growing late," Timothy John replied. "Come, let us begin," and they all sat down at the table with its ribbon streamers and best dishes, while Timothy John arranged Juniper under his parasol next to the ballerina.

"First we'll have ice cream," Maggie began.

"Ice cream?" Miss Christabel asked. "But we have no ice cream."

"Yes we do." Maggie set out three bowls and laid little spoons next to them. "It's butter pecan," she said, spooning from a larger bowl.

Timothy John and Miss Christabel bent over the table. "But the bowls are empty!" they both cried together.

"Well, it's pretend," Maggie answered. "Like the tea and the cream and sugar and all that."

"Pretend tea?" Miss Christabel asked. "Do we have pretend tea, Timothy John?"

Timothy John looked into the teapot. "No," he replied. "Not today. But perhaps I can find some for next time."

Maggie sighed. "Well, this is pretend ice cream," she said. "You have to make believe it's really there."

"Pretend ice cream," Timothy John said. "What an excellent idea. That keeps it from melting, Miss Christabel."

"It sounds very curious to me," Miss Christabel said. "I don't believe I've tasted anything pretend before. I hope it isn't bitter," and she hesitantly raised the spoon to her lips. "It has a familiar taste," she said after a pause, "but I can't quite place it. Let's give some to Juniper, too," and she held the bowl next to the dog's china nose. "Just *pretend* to eat it," she cautioned him.

"Is the cake pretend, too?" Timothy asked.

"No, the cake is real," and Maggie produced the little cupcake, inserting the candle into its hard crust of icing.

"That's too bad," Timothy John answered. "I seem to be developing a taste for pretend things."

"Well, it's real. And I brought real matches, too, so we can light the candle and sing 'Happy Anniversary.' "

She had never struck a match before, and she wasn't altogether sure how to go about it. Sweep it across the sole of your shoe, she remembered, but the match broke in two when she tried that, and she had to use another, this time holding her fingers closer to the head. Over and over she drew it across the bottom of her shoe, holding her breath, squeezing her eyes shut, so that when it finally did ignite, in a sudden hissing spurt, she let out a surprised cry of pain and dropped it on the table.

"It's a fire!" Timothy John and Miss Christabel jumped from the table. "It's another fire!" The paper shade of the parasol was by now a blade of flame, and in the next instant nothing remained of its red and purple blossoms but a scattering of ash clinging to its frail, blackened ribs. Juniper, knocked aside, lay upside down in a saucer. For a while nothing could be heard but the little clicking noises made by Miss Christabel's china hands as they shook together.

"Well," Timothy John finally said, standing Juniper upright again. "That was close, wasn't it?" and he looked around at Miss Christabel and Maggie.

"Close to what?" Miss Christabel asked, smoothing out her skirt.

But Maggie couldn't speak at all. She lifted the parasol's bare skeleton and let it drop again. The beautiful flowery sunshade was all gone. Now Juniper had no present, and she felt her throat tighten. "Poor Juniper," she tried to say, but no sound came.

"It can still be used," Miss Christabel said. "It can be a

transparent sunshade, for letting the sun *in*. When you want to take a sunbath, for example."

"A sunshade for sunbaths," Timothy John said. "What an excellent idea. If Juniper takes sunbaths, there's no need to buy him a washtub," and Juniper growled softly.

"But it's all gone," Maggie whispered. "The paper part with the flowers," and once more she felt a sting to her eyes.

"But the part that's left is quite nice," Timothy John said, brushing the blackened frame with his china hand. "It's like a little tree," and very carefully he stood it up. "Now," he went on, "isn't there a song that is sung at parties? Happy something?"

" 'Happy Anniversary,' " Miss Christabel said. "Sing it, Maggie."

Maggie opened her mouth and tried to sing. The words came out only in little spurts at first, but soon Timothy John began to beat time with the ice cream spoon and Miss Christabel to tap her foot loudly on the floor. "Happy Anniversary, dear Miss Christabel, Timothy John, and Juniper," Maggie managed to end in a jumble, "Happy Anniversary to you."

"That's a lovely song," Timothy John said. "You must teach me the words someday."

Then, with a small spoon, Maggie began to divide the hardened cupcake into little pieces. "First Juniper," she said, offering him a large crumb, "because his present got ruined.

And next Miss Christabel, then Timothy John, and now me."
She peeled off the paper pleating and sucked on its waxy
crumbs. The icing cracked under her teeth when she bit into
the cake itself, but she softened it under her tongue and
swallowed some of the pieces whole. At her next bite, though,
she saw that both dolls were staring at her, their cake pieces
poised in front of their lips. "That's a ridiculous way to eat,"
Timothy John said. "There's nothing left when you're done,"
and after that, she ate as they did, making little nibbling
noises with her lips and returning the cake to her plate as
she did with the wooden slices of bread.

At last they put their hands in their laps and sat back,
looking from one face to another. "That was very nice,"
Miss Christabel said.

"Let's promise something," Maggie said. "Let's promise
to have an Anniversary party like this every May fourteenth.
With ice cream and cake and a candle—only I won't light
it again—and streamers and presents and singing. And everything. Just like today."

"You forgot the games," Timothy John reminded her.

"Games!" exclaimed Miss Christabel. "We haven't played
games yet. What games do you know, Maggie?"

Maggie thought awhile. "Ghost," she finally suggested.
"Do you know ghost?"

Both dolls rose in alarm. "Ghost?" they cried.

"No, not the dead people kind of ghost," Maggie said.

"The spelling game. You know, first I say a letter and then you say a letter and you keep going around saying letters until someone spells out a word and that person gets G for ghost."

"And what do you do with it then?" Timothy John asked.

"With what?"

"With the G you get."

"Nothing." Maggie grew impatient. "Whoever gets G-H-O-S-T first loses."

"Loses what?"

"Loses the *game.*"

"But then it can't be played again until it is found."

"No, I mean loses like you don't win."

"It makes no sense."

"It's just a spelling game." Maggie shrugged. "It's supposed to teach you how to spell and stuff like that."

"I don't care for games that teach you things," Timothy John said. "You think you're having a good time, and all the while you're really learning something instead. Let's play that game—what was it, Miss Christabel? The one where someone puts a handkerchief over his eyes and tries to catch someone else?"

"Ah, that," Miss Christabel answered. "Remember that? Blindman's buff. What a wonderful game that was. All that bumping into things."

"Blindman's buff," Timothy John said. "Of course. Let's

play that now. I'll be blindman. Maggie, tie a napkin around my eyes so I can't see."

Blindman's buff. She had seen children play that in one of her old schools. She had never played, but she had always wondered what it felt like to move around a room, blindfolded, reaching into a tangle of taunting arms, catching nothing.

"Tie it so it won't slip down," Timothy John said as Maggie knotted a tea towel around his head. "Now scatter!" he ordered, and Miss Christabel swept to the other side of the room. Maggie watched as Timothy John stretched his hands in front of him and moved cautiously first in one direction and then, turning abruptly, in the other until he bumped into her knee. "Caught you!" he cried, pulling the blindfold down to his chin. "But you didn't move," he now said. "Why didn't you move?"

"I don't know," Maggie responded. "I was just watching."

"But you're supposed to move away when I come close," Timothy John told her. "Keep moving, or you'll be caught. Let's try it again," and he pushed the blindfold across his painted eyes. "Scatter!" he called out again, and this time Maggie tiptoed over to the other wall while Miss Christabel slipped across the room in her whispering skirt.

Once again he stretched his arms straight ahead and pushed slowly across the floor toward Miss Christabel. As he neared her she edged away, and in the next instant he would have crashed into the wall. "Look out!" Maggie cried aloud, and he spun around and headed for her knees. "Caught you!" he called out, stabbing at her with his china hands. "You shouldn't have spoken," he said, pulling down his blindfold.

"But you were about to bump into the wall."

"Of course I was," Timothy John answered. "That's the fun of it. And now it's your turn because you were caught. You're blindman. Miss Christabel, find a cloth for Maggie's eyes," and in a moment Maggie was wrapping one of the dolls' bed sheets around her own head.

At first everything was silent as she stood stiffly, seeing nothing but the maroon darkness behind her eyelids. Then, near her hem, she heard the rustle of a skirt and the creak of a knee joint, and she crouched down low, sweeping her hands back and forth. Once her knuckles hit a wall, and later something on the tea table fell over with a thin sound. Miss Christabel's skirt swished somewhere on the right and Maggie quickly grabbed with her hand, but she met only the wardrobe and she heard, now from the left, a tiny laugh. She put out her hands again. This was the table—no, the chair—and here was something hard and cold—the stove. Here was the clothes chest, and this must be the alcove with the broom. The creaking and rustling had gone silent. Where *were* they? Now there was a rustle, then footsteps, from where? Beyond the doll room and into the attic? "No fair going out of this room," she called out, but there came no answer. Suddenly there was a loud crash and then two thuds, and Maggie put her hand out again. "Caught you!" she cried out at last, bunching the folds of a silk dress in her hands. "Caught you!" She pulled her blindfold down and squinted into the blur of light. The dress she was clutching slowly came into focus and she stared at it. It was blue, not black, and it had no buttons. It was big and wide, not tiny, and it stretched far above Maggie's crouched form. Slowly she lifted her gaze until she found herself looking straight into the faces first of Aunt Harriet and then of Aunt Lillian.

Part IV

PROLOGUE

❧

And now the older one wanted to try on the purple dress and to set it whirling around her legs. "Can I wear the flower, too?" she asked. "Can I wear it in my hair so I'll look just like you at your aunts' party?"

"No," Maggie answered. "It will crumble."

"Then let me hold it. Just for a minute," she insisted. "I'll be careful," and she stood still as Maggie slowly placed the lilac, fragile as china lace, in her cupped hands. "Did everybody like your dress?" she asked, blowing softly on the blossom, watching it tremble, rocking it this way, that. "All those people at the Health Society meeting? Did they like how you had gained all that weight and how your hair got to look nice and everything? Did they like you?"

"I guess so," Maggie answered.

The sun had dropped low behind the house, and the lawn chair, upside down, sent a jungle gym of shadows across the prickly grass in the backyard. Maggie stood at the window, pressing her thumb against the glass, making spots and watching them fade.

"Did your aunts?" the older girl persisted. "Did they like how you looked?"

"I don't know. Probably. The dress was nice."

"Then how come they sent you away?" the little one wanted to know. She, too, was at the window now, measuring the top of her head against Maggie's arm. "How come if Aunt Harriet and Aunt Lillian liked the way you looked and everything and gave you a party, how come they sent you away?"

That was always the hardest question of all, and they asked it all the time—not because they liked her answer, but because they didn't, and they hoped that someday she would change it.

"I don't know," Maggie answered, as she always did. "They probably had other stuff to do," and she told them instead about saying good-bye to Barbara at school, about driving to the station with her aunts, and finally about what happened to Uncle Morris.

"Maybe that was why," the older sister said. "Because of what happened to Uncle Morris."

"But why would they want her to go away after that?" the little one objected. She was crying now, as she always did when Maggie got to the part about Uncle Morris. "I would think *they'd want her to stay then,"* she said, *wiping her nose with a knuckle and pressing her eye with the heel of a hand, "to keep them company."*

"No," Maggie answered quietly. "They didn't."

CHAPTER THIRTY

❦

"What *is* this? What are you doing here? What's burning?"
Aunt Harriet's foot stamped on the floorboards, and Maggie
slowly rose, straining against the cramps in her knees.

"Nothing," she answered, her voice a croak. She tried
to immobilize her aunt's eyes, to keep them from looking
around the room, but Aunt Harriet's gaze had already begun
to pull away, and Maggie's eyes followed, taking in the scene
as her aunt must be seeing it: a jumble of old doll furniture,
a knickknack dog in a worn basket, Aunt Harriet's own scarf
in red tatters, a pair of dolls facedown on the floor, a doll's
tea set, and—Maggie gasped at the sight—a mass of china
fragments on a small table.

"Lillian!" Aunt Harriet cried out. "Look at this! It's the Dresden figurine! It's smashed to pieces!"

Maggie stared at the remains of the ballerina—its slippered feet here, there; its lace frill a scatter of crumbs; its fingers a trail of chips, its face an open hole. She reached toward the table, but a hand pulled her back.

"The Dresden ballerina!" Aunt Lillian cried, and she joined Aunt Harriet at the table. "For over a hundred years," she said in a voice that Maggie could barely hear, "we have had that in the family, and in one minute it's gone. *Gone.*" Both aunts gazed down as though at a dead body, touching nothing, barely breathing.

Maggie could slip away now. Around the wardrobe she could go, across the floor, down the stairs, through the hall, out the house.

"What's this!" Aunt Harriet seized a match, another match, the blackened parasol frame. "Maggie!" and she whirled around. "Come back! What were you burning up here?"

"She was about to set the house on fire," Aunt Lillian exclaimed. "If we hadn't come up when we did, she would have—Harriet!" she cried out. "Look at your scarf! The Persian silk! It's torn to shreds!"

"Take her downstairs!" and in the next moment a hand gripped each of her shoulders and she was steered across the attic floor and down the narrow, dark steps, leaving behind her the two dolls playing dead on the floor, Juniper upside down in his basket, and the ballerina, the beautiful ballerina, scattered among the cake crumbs on the table.

The parlor stood empty. The guests were gone, but a semi-circle of folding chairs remained in front of the window, and empty teacups and plates rested here and there like shells on a beach. The two aunts seated Maggie on a chair against the wall and stood over her, side by side, a pair of giant birds about to invade their dinner.

They started out in very quiet voices, quiet and low—Aunt Harriet first. "How do you imagine it looked," she began, "when our guests arrived and you were nowhere to be seen?"

"What do you think it was like to have all our guests searching the house for you from top to bottom, and behind every tree in the garden?" Aunt Lillian continued.

"How do you think we felt when it came time to discuss the business of the day and the business of the day had disappeared?"

And although that was one of those questions no one was supposed to answer, Aunt Lillian answered it anyway. "Like fools," she said. "We felt like fools."

And now their voices began to rise. "You have betrayed us!" one cried.

"You have disobeyed!"

"You have vandalized!"

"You have committed arson!"

"You have committed larceny!"

Arson, larceny. Which was which? One was burning things down, the other was—what?—something about other people's wives. No. Stealing. She had stolen something. The ballerina. And the scarf.

"You took our most valuable heirloom and destroyed it!"

"You tore our clothing to shreds!"

"You nearly burned the house down!"

"After we took you in and cared for you all these months."

"We bought you a beautiful *dress!*" Aunt Harriet's voice grew shriller at each word, and when she came to "dress" it shattered altogether. People sounded like that before they began to cry, and Maggie wondered if her aunt's face would suddenly spatter with tears.

"We bought you a doll. A beautiful clean doll, brand-new, but you wouldn't touch it. You didn't play with dolls. And now we find you surrounded by rubbish playthings from a scrap heap."

"How do you know those toys hadn't belonged to some diseased child?"

"They're not dol—" Maggie began, but she fell silent. What were Timothy John and Miss Christabel doing right now in the attic? she wondered. Making up their minds, probably, that it was safe to get up. Just beginning to stir, probably, slowly shaking their Sunday clothes free of wrinkles and looking around. In a moment they would set Juniper right side up in

[268]

his basket, and then they would discover the ballerina lying in splinters on the tea table. "Mercy!" Miss Christabel would say, and Timothy John's hands would click together in distress.

"What is that in your sleeve?" Aunt Lillian demanded. "Look at this, Harriet. She's taken someone's handkerchief."

"Whose is it?" Aunt Harriet asked, and both women bent over the little square of cloth Miss Christabel had given Maggie.

"It's hand embroidered," Aunt Lillian said.

"It seems very old. Look how tiny it is. It must be Vera Burton's. She always carries a handkerchief. She must have dropped it when she was searching the rooms upstairs. Where did you get this handkerchief, Maggie?"

Maggie watched as the handkerchief was stretched and turned in her aunt's hands. "I found it," she said. "I found it on my way to school."

"Stolen," Aunt Lillian declared. "I'd know Vera Burton's handkerchief anywhere."

"I *found* it!" Maggie's voice rose to a shout, and she began to believe her own words, to picture the tiny embroidered handkerchief crumpled against a lamppost in front of the school building. She saw herself coming upon it suddenly one morning, a surprise, like a hidden burst of flowers unexpectedly blooming on the pavement. She saw herself picking it up, examining it, sniffing it, smoothing it out, rubbing it along her cheek, running her finger over the satin-smooth stitching of the roses, making it hers forever. "It's *mine!*" she shouted. "I *found* it!" But Aunt Harriet pressed it into her own hand, making it disappear behind her thumb like a coin in a magician's palm.

Maggie's eyes darted around the room, coming to rest at last on the two portraits over the mantel—the man's, the woman's. Isn't it mine? she wanted to ask, winning their support, but they only stared at her coldly.

"She's a common thief," Aunt Lillian said, but all of a sudden something in the picture caught Maggie's eye, and the voices of her aunts became only a jumble at her back as she advanced to the wall. "It's *hers*," she whispered, looking up at the woman on the canvas.

It *was* hers; the handkerchief that protruded from the lace cuff on the canvas bore the same grouping of roses with the same latticework of dark-green stems as the one now in Aunt Harriet's hand. That was where Maggie had seen the design before. On the painting. The handkerchief had belonged to the lady over the mantel.

"It's hers," she whispered again, and in the next moment she lunged at her aunt and scratched the little scrap of cloth out of her hand. "It's *hers!*" she shouted, crushing it into her own palm, and she ran from the room, along the hall, through the garden door, across the lawn, beyond the birches, past the roses, and into the border of woods at the far end of the garden.

CHAPTER THIRTY-ONE

✥

The woods were not woods at all. Not the kind of woods, that is, that all those fairy-tale creatures lived in—those acres of dense trees where bears and dwarfs and witches dwelled, and from which there was no exit ever. Looking over her shoulder, Maggie could still see her aunts' house clearly, but the tangle of branches and brush was heavy, and she was sure no one could see her. She slowed her pace now and rested against the trunk of a tree. She uncurled the little handkerchief and smoothed it over the hump of her knee. It had belonged to the lady in the picture; she had held it in her hand, touched it now and then to her face, tucked it into the frill of her sleeve. How, then, had Miss Christabel gotten hold of it? Did Miss

Christabel know about the lady in the picture?

Her cheeks burned with a dry heat, and her breath came in painful spurts. She looked back once again; no one had followed. The great lawn was empty, and the house, seen from this distance, belonged to some other season. Quiet and serene, it was like a picture hanging in some darkened hallway, and it offered no danger. She continued on.

Abruptly the woods ended, and she stood now in a large field. Strange that in all the months she had lived here she had never ventured beyond the broad lawn and the stand of birches.

The hour was growing late; it must be close to dinnertime, but the afternoon light still held, and she pressed forward, setting to flight with every step a cloud of soft insects. The field was a sea of gray weeds, with here and there a cluster of dandelion heads gleaming like a spill of coins. Nothing else—no house, no fence, no living creature—interrupted the landscape, and she thought for a moment that she had entered some private world where no one had ever stepped. So that when, suddenly bruising her toe and catching her breath in pain and surprise, she came upon the gravestones, it was as though she had been startled out of a dream.

There were two, and their surfaces were covered with turtle-green mildew. Maggie crouched down before one and squinted at its faint script. Along the top were the carved letters of a name. An O maybe, or a C. An indistinct P. Or

B. Something next. F? Two F's? The rest was rubbed away. Then there followed a verse. She could make out the words "day" and "say." Then numbers—dates they would be, or ages—and she pushed away the surrounding tufts of weed. Something struck her hand and a stain of blood, dark as an apple seed, sprang to her fingertip. She sucked it dry and pressed its pain against Miss Christabel's handkerchief. A bundle of slender rose branches, thick with thorns, lay in a heap among the weeds. Somebody, long ago, must have put roses on the graves. But whose graves? She bent toward the writing on the other stone and scratched at its mildew with her thumbnail.

All of a sudden a shadow fell across her hand, and she heard a step behind her. In an instant she was on her feet, facing Uncle Morris, his bowler set stiffly on his head, the silver knob of his walking stick catching a spark from the sun, a hand held behind his back.

"Maggie," he said. "How unusual that we should find each other in all this crowd. It's a good thing you were standing still, or I should never have caught sight of you at all."

Maggie stared at him. Had he been sent out to get her? Should she run? And what was that behind his back?

"But now that we have met," he went on, "we must stick together. We don't want to lose each other again."

Maggie sighed, tired now of his jokes.

"What a peculiar headdress your finger is wearing," he

observed after a while. "Is it a turban?"

Maggie looked down at the flowered handkerchief bunched around her finger. Had he been sent to retrieve it? "It's a handkerchief," she said, concealing it with her thumb. "I found it. On my way to school."

"A handkerchief for your finger. In case it has to blow its nose. I must remember to do that myself. My fingers are always getting sniffles at odd moments."

"I cut it," Maggie said. "My finger, I mean," she added, warding off another joke.

Uncle Morris put his head to one side. "Cut your *finger*? Why did you do that? Did you run out of paper?"

"I cut it on a thorn," she said. "There are some old roses over there in the weeds." She pointed behind her, not turning around.

"On a thorn? Ah, yes, thorns. Rose teeth. Do you know about rose teeth, Maggie? You must be very careful of them. Roses are especially fond of fingers, and they nibble at any that come their way. Ankles, too. There is nothing a rose likes better than a fine ankle with a thin layer of sock." At that he produced from behind his back a long spray of red roses, fragile and moist, in a cone of oily green tissue. "Most people make the mistake of looking at the petals, when it's the teeth that should be watched. Remember that when you help me," and he held out one of the slender green stems to her. Help him do what? Maggie looked at the rose but

[274]

did not take it. "Come," he urged, and he advanced to the two stones and laid a rose branch at each. "Here are yours," and he held the remaining flowers out to her.

"Who's buried here?" she asked, not moving. "What are you putting those roses here for?"

"Who's buried here?" Uncle Morris straightened out and turned to look her full in the face. "What a strange question. Didn't you know? Isn't that why you're here today?"

She waited for one of his jokes, but he didn't continue. "Know what?" she asked.

"Today is the anniversary of their death," he explained. "May fourteenth."

"Who?" she asked, catching her breath. "Whose death?"

"Theirs," he answered, looking puzzled. "The Greens."

The Greens? "That's who's buried here? The ones in the pictures?" She bent over and again examined the carved letters on the stone. That said Green? "Which one died today?" she asked. "I mean, which one's anniversary is it?"

"Both of theirs," Uncle Morris answered, kneeling down with his flowers. "They died the same day."

"They both died the same day? May fourteenth? That's when they both died? How come? How did they die?"

The rose branch at the right-hand stone had fallen over, and Uncle Morris stooped down to prop it up again before answering with the words Maggie knew he would now speak: "In a fire."

CHAPTER THIRTY-TWO

᪣

"Miss Christabel! Timothy John! I'm here! I came back!"
Maggie cried at the top of the stairs. "I finally came back!
Except I can't stay very long." She couldn't stay at all, really.
She had told her aunts she was going upstairs to the bathroom—they made her tell them wherever she went now—
and she had turned the water on in the sink and let it run
noisily while she stole up to the attic. "Here I am!" she
announced as she rounded the wardrobe. "And guess what!
I know who you are now. Uncle Morris told me. Well, he
didn't tell me exactly, but I guessed. You're—hey," she said,
advancing into the room.

Everything remained as she had left it when, a week earlier,
her aunts had steered her across the floor and down the stairs.

The streamers still hung in wide arcs along the walls and across the table edge, and the fragments of the ballerina made a little hill among the tea things. The two dolls lay sprawled on the floor precisely where they had fallen when Aunt Harriet and Aunt Lillian had entered the attic, and Juniper remained upside down in his basket.

"Hey," she repeated. "It's only me. It's Maggie. You can get up now," and she waited for them to stir. "Hey," she said after a while. "My aunts have gone. And anyway, we have to straighten up around here. The ballerina's all broken and there are cake crumbs all over the table. Your chair's knocked over, Miss Christabel, and the streamers should come down. Hey, come *on*."

The room stayed still.

She stepped over to Miss Christabel's form and knelt beside it. "It's time to get up," she said. "It's time for tea. Miss Christabel? Are you okay?" She laid the back of her fingers across the doll's china cheek as though testing for fever. "Miss Christabel?" She lifted the doll by its waist, but the china head only wobbled back and forth and the arms dangled uselessly at its side. "Miss *Chris*tabel!" The doll lay lifeless in her hands, and its painted smile was that of any doll on a shelf.

"Timothy John?" she said, whirling now to the other doll. She picked him up and shook him too, but he made no reply and only swung aimlessly from her hand while the new braided tie flapped back and forth like a loose banner in the wind.

Her eyes moved to the table where Juniper lay among the cake crumbs and the ballerina fragments. His ear was missing again. "Juniper?" she called out, seizing his china form. "*Ju*niper!" She shook him as though he were a watch that refused to tick, and held him to her ear, but no answer came.

She sat back on her heels, resting her hands on her knees and looking from one doll's body to the other. Now and then she sighed. All at once she sat up. "Hey, how about some tea?" she said, getting to her feet. "Some nice hot tea. *That's* what you need. Tea. With all those vapors and everything. That'll wake you up," and she carried the kettle to the stove. "I'll get some bread and butter, too. You haven't eaten anything in a long time. That's what's the matter with you. You're weak. You—you haven't taken any nourishment," she said. "You haven't taken any nourishment in—in your *sys*tem. You're all—you're all skin and bones. Look at you. Here, I'll get it ready. I just have to pour it in the teapot and put the cozy on to keep it warm. And then I'll get the cups ready and everything, and the cream and sugar. You first, Miss Christabel," and in another moment she was crouching over the woman doll's body, cradling the china head in her elbow and holding the teacup against the painted mouth. "Here," she whispered. "Drink it. It will wake you up. Just *taste* it, then, if you don't want to drink it. Just one taste . . . *taste* it!" she shouted, but the doll lay limp in her arms, and Maggie finally let it roll onto the floor.

"You, then, Timothy John. Taste the tea. *Just one taste!*" and she held the empty cup to his face. "Taste it! What's the *matter* with you? Make those noises you used to make when we had tea. *Drink it!*" she shouted. "Juniper, *you* drink it," and she shoved the teacup against the dog's china nose. "*Drink it!* Make noises. *Do* something!"

And then she remembered the words of the two dolls when she had asked about bringing a visitor to the attic.

"But you must never do that! We must never be seen!"

"Why not?" she had asked.

"Because something dreadful would happen," Timothy John had answered. Something like that, and Miss Christabel had silenced him.

They *had* been seen, by her two aunts, who had discovered them after Maggie, in her haste to reach the birthday party, had forgotten to close behind her the closet door of the empty room. And now—was this the dreadful thing that would happen? Would they . . . could dolls *die*?

Maybe they had just passed out or something. From fright. Maybe they needed air. There was a poster in the school nurse's office that showed how to do mouth-to-mouth resuscitation—black-and-white drawings of a cartoon man with his mouth pressed against the cartoon face of an outstretched figure on a beach. A little balloon over the man's head contained the words "Exhale, two, three, four. Inhale, two, three, four." Maggie might try that. She could breathe air into Miss Christabel's painted mouth until, in a sudden miracle, the china arms would twitch with life, the legs in their little black boots would slowly bend, and the doll would stand upright like the cartoon figure in the last drawing on the poster. For a quick moment Maggie put her lips to the doll's face and breathed deeply, but nothing happened, and she wiped the china taste from her mouth. It was a stupid idea, anyway. Dolls didn't breathe.

For a long while she stood in the stillness of the room, doing nothing, staring at the two china bodies lying in their crumpled clothes on the floor and at Juniper standing like an ornament on the table. Her own breathing was the only sound to touch her ear. Inhale, two, three, four, she said in her head. Exhale, two, three, four.

"Hey," she finally said in a small whisper. "Miss Christabel, your dress is all wrinkled," and very carefully she lifted the doll from the floor. "Here," she said. "Let me straighten it out. And your new shawl. It's all crooked from where you fell." She laid the doll across her knee, smoothing out its clothes and tidying its hair as well. "And your hands are dusty," she added, taking Miss Christabel's hard, cold hand in her own and wiping it clean with the edge of her skirt.

"And you, Timothy John," she said, turning next to him. "You need to be fixed up too." She rearranged his suit so that the sleeves were even and the pants unwrinkled, and she tugged at the ends of his braided tie. "There," she said, curving the little gold watch chain across his stomach, "you're all better. And now, and now, it's time for everyone to come to the table. Come on," and she propped both dolls in their chairs and installed Juniper in his basket on the floor.

"First I have to clean up around here," she said. "There's a whole bunch of broken pieces on the table, china and stuff, and I have to sweep it into the coal scuttle. On top of the broken teacup. Remember the broken teacup, Miss Christabel?" And then, changing her voice, she answered for the doll: "Yes, I remember." "Cream and sugar, Miss Christabel?" she asked in her own voice, and then, speaking for the doll: "Thank you, I will." She held the empty cup to Miss Christabel's mouth and made sipping noises for her. "Timothy John? Will you have some tea?" and she answered for him, too, in a low voice: "Yes, please." "Juniper?" She placed a saucer against his nose under the table and made a little growl in her throat. "Bread and butter?" she asked the two dolls, and then, "How lovely," she answered for them in their voices, and she made little nibbling noises as she held the wooden slices against their mouths. "How thoughtful of you to give us bread and butter," she said for Timothy John. "It is just what we needed. We were faint from hunger."

"Maggie always gives us everything we need," she said for Miss Christabel. "She is our caretaker."

"We are lucky to have her here," she answered for Timothy John.

She should go soon. Her aunts would begin to wonder where she was, and soon they would knock on the door of the empty bathroom with the water running uselessly in the sink. They might follow her up here, now that they knew the way, and then confine her to her room. They might throw away the dolls and all the doll things. They might send her away. She would go down in a minute. Two minutes.

First, though, she would mark the exact point where the dolls' hands lay on the tablecloth. She had done something like that once with a dead turtle. It had been her roommate's turtle, and one day it had stopped moving and a brown trickle had appeared on its shell every time it was pressed. "It's dead," Maggie had said, but her roommate said no, it was only napping, so they placed it on the windowsill and outlined its nose with a pencil line. They made themselves stay away for five hours, and when they returned, the turtle's nose still rested like a stone on the pencil mark, and they buried him in the back garden. Maggie would try that now with the dolls. She would place their fingertips at the very edge of the bread slabs with the teacups lined up perfectly at their wrists. Then she would stay away for a long time. Longer than five hours. For a day. Three days. A week. At the end of a week she would come back, and if they hadn't moved, she would— What would she do?

"I have to go now," she said to the doll bodies propped in their chairs, and she placed the little newspaper in Timothy John's lap. "Here," she said. "You can read this while I'm gone."

"Ah, the newspaper," she said in Timothy John's voice. " 'Two Lost in Fire,' it says."

"Pity." She made her voice high now. "Two what, I wonder."

And now a low voice for Timothy John: "Gloves, maybe. Two gloves."

"No, it wasn't gloves, Timothy John," she said in her own voice. "It was people. Two people. And I even know their name. It was Green." Very carefully she straightened their lifeless forms at the tea table and lined up their fingertips along the sides of the bread. "They had this school downstairs," she continued, pushing Miss Christabel's chair in to keep her from toppling to one side, "and they used to sleep in the empty room, except it wasn't empty then, and one day they went to the barn to burn a whole bunch of papers and stuff in the stove, and the whole barn burned down with them in it. And their dog, too. They had a dog. They all died together. On the same day. May fourteenth."

After a long silence she spoke for each of the dolls. "Imagine that," she said in Timothy John's low voice, and then "Mercy!" in Miss Christabel's high whisper.

CHAPTER THIRTY-THREE

❧

June now, and the birch leaves hung over her head like a swarm of green butterflies in the hot air. Carefully she sat down, fitting her legs into the shadow of a tree trunk and laying her fingers in the outline of a branch.

She was to be sent away soon; her aunts had just told her that that morning. Sent away for good. "You have been a great disappointment to us," Aunt Harriet had said. She and Aunt Lillian had sat side by side like two chess pieces on the square sofa cushions in the parlor, and Maggie had sat opposite, wetting a length of hair under her tongue.

"You have failed us," Aunt Lillian put in, while Maggie painted the edge of her cheek with the wet brush of her hair.

"You are an unwholesome child."

Maggie's eyes wandered, as they always did now when she was in the parlor, to the portraits over the mantel, and she picked out their familiar details—the line of buttons down the woman's black dress, the handkerchief with its cluster of roses, the spotted dog at the man's feet, the threadlike curve across the man's stomach—his watch chain, she now knew. And the watch, the concealed gold watch, what hour did it announce? What time did it say in the folds of the dark painted pocket? Eight thirty-five?

The two aunts continued to speak, but Maggie's eyes were on the watch chain still, and it wasn't until later that their final words in the parlor organized themselves in her head and took on meaning: "And so we are looking for a suitable place for you to live. You will be informed when arrangements have been made."

In a little while, at exactly four fifteen, in fact, her week away from the attic would be up, and she would steal back upstairs to see if the dolls had moved beyond the barrier she had made of bread slabs and teacups.

Just one *inch*. That's all they would have to have moved. One inch, and she would know they were still alive. Half an inch. It would take a while, maybe, but then, little by little—a turn of the wrist one day, a bend of the elbow the next—they would return to life, until one day they would push back their chairs and walk across the room and speak her name once more. One inch, she said. That's all. Move one inch. *Move!*

When you want to wish for something very hard, the girls in school said, close your eyes and don't cross anything— not your fingers, not your toes, not anything—or your wish won't come true. Maggie straightened her fingers against the ground and her toes inside her shoes. Not even your *hair*, they warned, and she separated the wet ropes of her hair along her cheek. Move, she said to herself, concentrating her wish behind tightened eyelids. Move, move, move. Just one *inch.*

The barn that had burned down had stood on the spot where she now rested. Uncle Morris had told her that. "What fire? Where?" she had asked as they had stood by the gravestones, and he had answered, as she knew he would, "In the barn."

"What barn?" she had pressed him further. "Where?" He had pointed then through the dense barrier of trees toward the house. "You can't miss it," he had answered. "It's the one that's not on the lawn anymore."

"*Where?*" Maggie had stamped her foot in exasperation. "Where was it before it burned down?"

"Exactly where it was *after* it burned down."

"WHERE?" and she expected another evasive reply, but instead he led her through the woods, across the lawn, and over to the small crowd of birches where, long ago, she had laid out the little rooms with twigs and where, before she discovered the dolls, she had listened to them speak. "Here it is," he said. "Or isn't, actually."

This was where the barn had been? Right here, where the birches were? Her birches? This is where the barn had burned down? Here?

By now she knew, too, about the fire in the barn and how it had started. Two nights ago, after her aunts had sent her to bed, she had silently crept along the upstairs hall and into the old schoolroom, crouching beside the shelves until she found what she was looking for—the bound diary with the writing pale as insect legs.

The light was dim, and she had to follow with her finger the strange words that stretched in slanted rows across each page. The book began abruptly, without title or name, with a date and two sentences, and Maggie sat down at one of the old wooden desks to read them.

"September 15

"Only seven girls enrolled so far this year.

"Dora will give us trouble and Alice is sickly."

But it was the last written page, halfway through the volume, that interested Maggie most, and she riffled the pages with her thumb until she reached it.

"May 14," it began.

"It is very quiet here now, with the girls all away, and there are old school papers to burn. I wonder if the stove

in the barn will take them. The door keeps falling off and"—
something, something; a watery stain here washed out the
words—"I must try to mend it."

That was the end. The remainder of the book was blank.

Maggie didn't return to her room that night until long
after her aunts had gone to bed, and she moved, silent as a
moth, along the wall of the darkened corridor, hearing in
her head, over and over, the words: "The door keeps falling
off. I must try to mend it."

The twigs that had outlined the little rooms on the ground
were now in disarray, and Maggie could no longer tell where
the kitchen belonged, or the dining room. She gathered them
all up in a bunch and swept them back and forth across the
grass, back and forth, making ripples, waves, ripples again.

"Ooh, what's that?" The Backwoods Girls stood at silent
attention in a semicircle at the edge of the birches. "What's
that you have?"

"It's a special thing I invented," she answered, holding
up the clutch of sticks. "It's a comb for grass. It makes the
grass all smooth. Don't step there—you'll mess it all up."

"Ooh, how wonderful. Can I try the comb, too? Can I?
Can I? Can I?"

"No. You wouldn't know how to work it. Only I know
how. It's very difficult."

"Ooh, what else is that in your hand?"

"This? It's a handkerchief. It's very old. It has all this embroidery on it and everything, and it's very valuable. Somebody gave it to me to keep and I'm not allowed to let anybody else touch it or anything. Here, I'll hold it up so you can see," and she pulled the square cloth taut before her face.

"Wonderful," somebody said, but it wasn't the Backwoods Girls. Quickly she lowered her arms and found Uncle Morris standing in front of her, his long shadow joining those of the tree trunks along the grass. "A wonderful way to dry the laundry," he went on, brushing the bowl of his hat on his sleeve. "Hold it up and breathe on it. How economical. But how do you manage with the sheets?" The next moment he was sitting at her side, letting the shadows of the trees lap over his legs.

There was a long silence, and then, finally, she said, "Tell me about the people in the pictures. Over the mantel."

"Ah, the people in the pictures," he replied at once. "Of course. Well, to begin with, they live in the parlor, as you might have noticed, in frames. They are next-door neighbors, and yet they never speak to one another. The man's chief occupation is to serve as a headrest for his dog. The dog, on the other hand, spends *his* time being a footrest for the man. I have always suspected, though, that when no one is looking they reverse positions. And clothing as well, so that what you take to be a man is in reality a dog wearing a dark suit and a watch chain across his chest. And what you recognize as a dog is in fact a man crouching in a fur coat, but I've never been able to prove that. The woman spends *her* days keeping a handkerchief warm in her sleeve. She—"

"What did they use to be like?" Maggie interrupted. "When they had the school and everything?"

"People in pictures never used to be anything. And they never had the school. The school had *them*—over the mantel."

"No, I mean the *real* people. Not the ones in the pictures. The Greens, who founded the school. What were they like? What did they do? What did they use to say?"

"Oh, *those.* I never knew them. They died long before I was born." He wasn't going to tell her anything, but it didn't matter. She already knew, and she remained silent a long time, listening to the birch leaves brush one another like soft wings overhead.

Suddenly she turned to him and seized his arm. "Make them come back," she whispered fiercely into his face. "Please. Make them come back."

"Ah," he answered, looking into the sky. "Make them come back. I am often quite successful at making things come back. Clouds, for instance. Clouds frequently come back if I urge them to, although they usually take their time about it. That one up there—see it? The one that looks like a bathrobe? I asked that one to come back last August, and here it is at last."

Maggie tightened her grip on his arm and shook it. "I mean *them*," she whispered, not taking her eyes from his face. "Make *them* come back."

For a long while Uncle Morris didn't answer at all. He only looked down at her, and neither of them spoke. "Please," she whispered again.

"Ah, them," he finally said. "Of course. Of course I'll make them come back." There was a new firmness to his voice and a sound of promise. "Of course I will. When it's time."

He knew, then. He *knew*, and Maggie smiled at him a little, the first smile she had ever offered him. Uncle Morris was the one who would make the dolls come back. "Of course I will," he had said—*promised*, almost. Timothy John and Miss Christabel might even now be shifting in their seats at the table, reaching out with their hands, knocking over the unsteady wall of wooden bread, brushing against the teacups. And Juniper would be just starting to growl in his basket. She must remember to fix his ear.

"When?" she asked. "When will it be time?"

Uncle Morris slipped his legs out from one shadow and under another. "When will it be time?" he repeated. "Well, it will be time tomorrow and the day after and the day after that, as well. There are very few moments, in fact, when it is not time. Right now," and he inspected his watch, "the time is four fifteen, but chances are that won't last more than five minutes, ten at the most—where are you running off to?"

No sound came from above as Maggie mounted the stairs, two at a time, and the creak of the floorboards was the only noise to enter her ears as she crossed the attic floor. She closed her eyes and held her breath as she rounded the wardrobe, whispering over and over, "Be alive, be alive, be *alive*," but in a single glance she saw that nothing had changed in the doll room at all. Miss Christabel's and Timothy John's fingertips rested precisely against the wall of wooden bread; their painted faces stared, unseeing, across the table; and Juniper lay like a stone in the basket where she had laid him seven days before, almost to the minute.

CHAPTER THIRTY-FOUR

❧

Red, black, red, black, red, black. Red jack on black queen, black ten on red jack, red nine on black ten, black eight on red nine. Maggie moved the cards about on her bed, making little piles of hearts, of clubs. She was going to lose the game— she had, in fact, lost it already—but she continued to count out the cards in her hand by threes, staring at them and turning them aside unused.

In a little while, in a minute, she would go downstairs and ask Uncle Morris the question she had been wanting to ask all along: "Do you know Timothy John and Miss Christabel?" That was exactly how she would put it. "Do you know them?" And then she would await his reply.

All morning she had been rehearsing the words before

the mirror. "Do you know Timothy John and Miss Christabel?" and the white face with the damp streaks of hair at each cheek would answer yes. "Yes, I know them," it would say carefully, holding her eyes in its own. Or, "No," it would answer, letting its eyes slide away. "Who?" Or something else: "Ah, Timothy John and Miss Christabel. Of course. Aren't they those two cats that live on the next street? The ones with the black stockings on their tails?"

But she would persist. "No, Uncle Morris. You know who I mean. Tell me. Tell me if you know them. Tell me, tell me, tell me. You said you'd bring them back. You promised. When it's time, you said. Well, it's time now," and she stared hard at the eyes in the mirror until, remembering something about people hypnotizing themselves, she looked away.

He would be downstairs by now. Her aunts had invited him the week before. "We will continue our discussion next Sunday," Aunt Lillian had said. "Precisely at three."

"Ah," he had answered. "Precisely at three."

The two aunts had spent that entire afternoon discussing Maggie with him—describing her, really—while she stood in the hall.

"She is skin and bones again."

"She sucks her hair."

"She doesn't speak."

"Her face is drawn."

"Her face is drawn?" Uncle Morris had interrupted.

"*Drawn?* How very odd. I always thought it was molded out of clay. Drawn," and there was a pause. Then: "Did they use colored pencils, do you suppose, or charcoal?"

"Morris!" Aunt Harriet snapped. "There is no point in your remaining here if you are not going to take this subject seriously," and Aunt Lillian told him to return next week. Today. Precisely at three.

It was past three now, and in a moment Maggie would find Uncle Morris in the parlor chair facing the two aunts on their sofa. Aunt Harriet would be speaking, and then Aunt Lillian would say something else, and Uncle Morris would say nothing.

She gathered the cards into a single stack and carried them downstairs. "Where's Uncle Morris?" she asked in surprise, looking around and seeing no one but Aunt Lillian seated at her desk, writing a letter. Writing about me, Maggie thought. To the new family—to warn them.

"Where's Uncle Morris?" she repeated, but Aunt Lillian continued to lean over her desk, and when she finally answered she didn't look up.

"He's gone," she said.

Maggie crossed to the chair in front of the portraits and laid the cards facedown on her lap. Could you play solitaire on your lap? Probably not, but she would try anyway. "Where'd he go?" she asked, spreading her skirt out and balancing the cards on her knees, but it wasn't until the cards were all laid out in order that Aunt Lillian finally lifted her face.

Whenever Maggie looked back on that moment, she saw it in changing patterns of black and red: the black and red of the two portraits as her eye spun past them; the black and red of the cards as they fell, helter-skelter, from her lap; the black of Aunt Lillian's dress and the oval of red lips that framed the words she spoke when she finally looked up from her desk. Aunt Lillian hadn't been writing after all, Maggie noticed; she had only been leaning her forehead into her palm. "Where'd he go?" Maggie asked, louder this time.

"He's gone," Aunt Lillian repeated in a faint voice.

"Gone where?"

"Away." Aunt Lillian's face was the color of the gray parlor walls and her eyes were large and staring. Maggie felt a rush of liquid flow through her arms and legs. "What do you mean, gone?" she asked.

"Gone," Aunt Lillian said, and then, after a pause, "forever," and she rose and crossed to the window, saying nothing further. Her back, like the cards lying facedown on the floor, was straight and unrevealing.

"What do you mean, gone," Maggie tried again, "forever?" You mean he's dead? she wanted to ask, but the word stuck like a scrap of wet paper in her throat.

Aunt Harriet was in the room now. She, too, wore black, and she took up her position at the other window. Maggie stared at the two black figures, standing as still as the large stone urns on the steps out front. In time a sob came, a breath was caught, and there was silence again before Maggie finally ran from the room.

She had a nosebleed halfway through the funeral. A nosebleed into a handkerchief held by a hand in a black glove. More red, more black. The widening red stain in the handkerchief was the most vivid picture she had of the entire occasion. It was, in fact, the *only* picture she had of the occasion. Her eyes had been closed the rest of the time.

It's a dream, she had told herself as she was being steered out of the house, down the stone steps, along the front walk, into a car. It's just a dream. It's one of those dreams where you know you're dreaming, but you can't wake yourself up. If I close my eyes, I won't see the dream and it will stop. Or it will just go on without me. Can that happen? Can dreams go on by themselves if there's nobody there to watch them? Can you make a dream stop by pretending to ignore it? I'll try that. I'll just sit here with my eyes closed and I won't move. I'll keep my head still and my lips together, she said, as someone led her out of the car, across a pavement, up some new steps, into an enclosed space, onto a wooden bench.

I'll just keep my eyes shut and wait for the dream to die. And then after a while I'll wake up and it will be time to go to school. There was a man's voice now, reciting something. A poem. No, a thing from the Bible. I'll cover my ears. Maybe when I wake up I'll find that *all* of this is a dream—Adelphi Hills, Aunt Harriet, Aunt Lillian, Uncle Morris. I'll find that I really live somewhere else. Maybe where I used to live a long time ago, with a mother and father.

Now there was the smell of flowers, spicy like cloves. Carnations or something, and she breathed through her mouth. What if she fell asleep in her dream? What if she fell asleep and dreamed another dream? Can you do that? Can you dream that you're dreaming? What if that dream was worse than this one? . . . Can you get locked into a dream forever and never wake up from it? Does your dream go on after you die? Is Uncle Morris dreaming now? Is he dreaming of me?

I'll count to a hundred. I'll just sit here with my eyes closed and my ears covered until a hundred is up. Five hundred. Then I'll open my eyes for a split second and see if the dream is still on. Seven hundred. When I open my eyes, I bet I'll find myself in the parlor or in school or something.

One. Two. Three. Four. Five . . .

Someone pulled her hand from her ear. The other hand.

"She's an ill-behaved child," she heard.

"Poor training."

"Bad nutrition."

"Look out, her nose is bleeding!" and suddenly her head was jerked back, a warm taste of vinegar seeped into her throat, and a slab of something cold was pressed to the back of her neck. Six. Seven. Eight. Nine . . . Her head was pushed forward now, and at last she opened her eyes and saw the red stain spreading across the white handkerchief held by the hand in a black glove. Blood. Her blood. Real blood, and she knew that she hadn't been dreaming at all, that Uncle Morris was dead, that she was attending his funeral, and that later in the day she would enter a house that would be empty of his presence forever. She knew, too, that he had not kept his promise after all. It was time for him to bring the dolls back, and all he had done was die.

Uncle Morris dead. Dead of a heart attack, somebody said. How could people like Uncle Morris die? she wondered, back again at Adelphi Hills. Here were the table, the books, the chairs, the mantel, the china cabinet, whose surfaces he had brushed, fingered, altered. Here was the air he had breathed, and here were the walls that had received his tall and clumsy shadow. How could he be dead?

She moved from the parlor into the hall. Here was the rack that had suspended his coat, and here was the mirror that had framed his head. Would he be there now, in the mirror? Could he? Cautiously, she peered in. There was her own face, white and solemn like a fish in a bowl, and over her shoulder, where Uncle Morris might have stood, a single object hung like a giant pearl at the end of a fishing line—

the light pull that he had hidden over and over on the ledge above the door.

With a sudden violent yank Maggie tore its string from the ceiling and ran with it up to her room. All afternoon and into the night, she sat on her bed staring at the smooth oval on its cord, rolling it back and forth like an egg across her palm, stroking it now and then with her finger, and, in time, splashing it with the tears that finally fell from her eyes. How could he be dead?

CHAPTER THIRTY-FIVE

❧❦❧

It didn't take Maggie long to empty her desk on the last day of school. All she had to do was gather the loose papers together, tap them into an even rectangle, roll them into a slender tube, and drop them in the wastebasket. That left only a scattering of paper reinforcements, dry and curled, some snips of lace left over from Miss Christabel's shawl, and a few paper clips, all pulled out of shape. She swept them all up with the edge of her hand and dropped them, too, into the wastebasket.

"What's your summer address?" Barbara had already emptied her desk and scrubbed its surface, and she was standing next to Maggie with a pen and a small notebook balanced on her pile of loose-leaf papers.

"My summer address?"

"Yeah. Here, write it down in this book. I'll write to you from camp."

"I don't have a summer address."

"You mean you're staying home all summer?"

"I'm moving. I'm going to live with somebody else."

"With somebody else? Who? Is it those people you visit with the roses and everything?"

"No. Some other people. A family. They have these two girls. Far away someplace."

"Far away? You mean you're not coming back to school next year?"

"No."

"When are you going?"

"Tomorrow."

"Tomorrow?" Barbara looked at her a long time. "You never even got to see my costume dolls," she said.

"No," Maggie answered. "That's okay. I don't play with dolls anyway."

"I came to say good-bye," Maggie said.

Timothy John and Miss Christabel continued to stare blankly across the table at one another, and Juniper sat in his basket on the floor. "I'm leaving tomorrow," she continued. "I'm going to live somewhere else with these other people. Far away."

She swiveled Miss Christabel's face toward her own and spoke for her. "Going away?" she said in a high voice. "But you can't go away. We need you here."

"Yes," Maggie answered. "Well, maybe I'll come back and visit sometime. I don't know."

"But we need you here all the time," she said for Miss Christabel. "We need you to take care of us, isn't that right, Timothy John?"

Maggie nodded Timothy John's head for him. "Yes," she made him say. "You are our special friend, Maggie. We think you are the most wonderful person ever. We like you a whole lot, and we don't want you to leave us. We need you here. We . . . we *love* you, Maggie."

"I love you, too," Maggie answered. "I love you both, and Juniper, too." She picked up both lifeless dolls, along with the china dog, and put them all in her lap. She rocked them all back and forth, the way she had seen mothers rock babies. "And I'm never going to forget you." She rested her chin on their reddish wigs and closed her eyes. "Ever," she whispered. Then she was silent for all of them as she held them close and watched as the sunlight moved across the table, touching the kettle with a sudden flash and settling finally on the faces of the dolls in her lap.

"Here," she said after a while. "Look. This is what I'll do. I'll fix you so that you can all look at each other and have tea together after I've gone away. It will be just like always." She smoothed Miss Christabel's dress and arranged her carefully at her place in front of the teacup and saucer.

"Here's your bread and butter, right where you can reach it," she added, "and I'll put the tea cozy on the teapot to keep it warm. For always."

"For always," she answered for Miss Christabel. "How nice."

"And now you, Timothy John." She seated him on the chair opposite and straightened his legs out. "You'll have to do the pouring from now on, now that I won't be here anymore," and she rested his hand on the teapot.

"Of course," she made him answer. "I love to pour."

"And Juniper can sit where you can both see him." She set the little basket on the table between the two dolls. "I forgot to look for your ear, Juniper. It probably got swept into the coal scuttle with the cake crumbs. Do you mind a whole lot, having only one ear? It's okay, really. You look nice, anyway. And here's a saucer for you to sip from, when you get hungry." She rumbled an answer for him. "Oh, and here's your newspaper, Timothy John, in case you want to read about the fire and the washtub." Then she knelt at the table and looked from one to the other.

"Maggie!" Someone was calling from downstairs.

"I have to go now," Maggie whispered, and she slowly rose. "Good-bye, Miss Christabel," and she put her hand on the doll's small head.

"Good-bye, Maggie," she answered for the doll.

"And you, Timothy John. Good-bye." She brushed his cheek with her knuckles and lowered her voice for his reply: "Good-bye, Maggie. We will think of you while you are gone."

"Maybe I'll come back someday," she said. "For a visit. And see you all. Good-bye, Juniper," and she ran her finger along the hump of his back.

"Good-bye," she said again when she reached the top of the steps, but this time she didn't answer for them, and she went downstairs with only the echo of her own voice in her ear: Good-bye.

CHAPTER THIRTY-SIX

❧

The bulky things went into the duffel bag first: shoes, coat, sweaters, skirts. Then the flat things: underwear, socks, pajamas, shirts. On top of these, smoothed out and folded into even thirds—the purple party dress, its velvet ribbon laid across the bodice in a soft loop. Finally the odds and ends: deck of cards, pen, comb and brush, toothbrush, sliver of soap wrapped in waxed paper. The lilac blossom, dried now and powdery. The light pull.

Quickly Maggie opened and shut the drawers of the dresser and of the little desk. They were all empty. Everything was empty. The closet was empty, the floor under the bed was empty, the window seat was empty, the sink was empty. The room was as bare as it had been the day when, nine months earlier, she had first set foot in it. Barer. When she had first arrived there had been layers of underwear in the dresser, a row of dresses on the closet pole, and, on the window seat, a doll whose pretty rubber face she had pushed in with her thumb.

She crossed over to the sink and looked in the mirror at the face that, in less than a day, the new family would see for the first time. What would she look like to them? White cheeks, damp hair, sharp chin, pale lips. Skin and bones again. Maybe the new family wouldn't like her. Maybe they would send her somewhere else.

"I'm going on a plane," she told the Backwoods Girls, who had just filed into the room and now stood around her bed.

"A plane? What's a plane?" they all asked.

"A plane is this big, special machine that you go inside and it flies in the air."

"Flies in the air! Ooh, how wonderful. Like a bird?"

"Yes, but it's as big as a boat, and you go inside it, and it takes you far away."

"Ooh, how wonderful. Can we go, too?"

"No, of course not. You're too dumb and poor. They wouldn't even let you on." But the Backwoods Girls would probably keep her company wherever she went, especially now. "Well, maybe," she said. "Maybe I can get you on."

"Maggie!" Aunt Harriet called from downstairs. In a few

minutes it would be time to leave for the train that would take her to the city with the airport. Aunt Harriet and Aunt Lillian were to drive her to the station, following the same route she and Uncle Morris had traveled the day she arrived, only this time in reverse, with the huge stone building that looked like a prison growing smaller and smaller behind her back, and the bare countryside filling gradually with stores and houses. She wondered if she would throw up again.

There was still room in the top of the duffel bag for something else. She looked around the empty room and then stood without moving for a long moment. She could, if she wanted, take the dolls. Fly upstairs and grab Miss Christabel and Timothy John and Juniper, and lay them on top of the soap and the toothbrush. Pull the cord tight around the neck of the duffel bag, covering their white china faces, and carry them all to wherever she was going.

She could set them up on the bed in her new room, far away, and whisper to them whenever she was alone. "Remember the roses, Miss Christabel?" she could say. "Mercy, yes," she would answer for Miss Christabel, and she would move Timothy John's head up and down as he remembered, too.

A stray sock was caught in the sheet at the foot of the bed, and she dropped it into the duffel bag. No, she wouldn't take the dolls. She would leave them just as they were, forever seated opposite each other at the table, each on the verge of speaking, with Juniper between them, ready at any moment to sip from the saucer at his basket. She would take that scene with her, holding it in her mind as carefully as if it were balanced on a tea tray, and create from it a haunting dream:

Someday—fifty years from now, a hundred—some other girl, some other "right one," would arrive at Adelphi Hills and make her way reluctantly along the front walk to a building she would mistake for a prison. A small red head would appear, or seem to appear, from some distant window, but she would remember it only later when, now in the parlor, now in the hall, faint scrapings, tiny whispers, stray words would nudge at her ear and make her pause over her book. In time there would be voices—a man's, a woman's—that only she could hear, and they would speak of fires and washtubs, of a dog. One day they would call her name.

"Emma!" they would cry, or, "Rose! Come! It is time!" and she would fly through the halls, opening doors, shutting them, until she found at last the hidden panel in the closet leading to the attic stairs. Then, carefully at first, stepping and pausing, she would pull herself up, stopping in front of the massive furniture in its white draperies, inching her way across the attic floor, shrinking at the sound—from where?— of a shattering cup, reaching the wardrobe, stopping, listening, and bursting all at once on the startling scene of two china dolls at a tea table turning their painted smiles at her and crying, "She's here! She's here at last!"

EPILOGUE

The sunlight had left the backyard, and the single lawn chair lay in the shadows like the skeleton of some giant insect. The day was over. The purple dress, lifeless now, lay across the bed in the darkening room, and the dried lilac rested on the dresser like a curl of lavender dust.

The Anniversary had come and gone and no one here had known about it. Soon Maggie would eat dinner with the two little sisters and their parents—her parents. After that she would get ready for bed, and the day would have slipped by like every other.

Back at Adelphi Hills, too, the Anniversary would be drawing to a close. The patch of sun would already have gone from the garden, leaving the wicker chairs and the wallpaper roses in deepening shadow, and the faces in the dining room would have grown dim as well.

"Will you always be our sister?" That was Edith, the older one. She always asked that. "Will you?" She ran her fingernail across the velvet ribbon, making pale rivers.

"Yes, of course."

"Always, always?"

"Yes."

"Even when you die?"

"Yes, of course, but that's silly." Maggie made a little braid out of Edith's hair, not fastening it, watching the strands loosen and fall apart.

"That's nice," said the little one—Clara. "That's nice that you'll be our sister always, even when you die." She began to sob aloud about Uncle Morris, as she always did, but Maggie, as she always did, said not to. "Don't cry," she said. "It's okay. It's okay that he died."

But she didn't say why it was okay. To do so would be to tell about the other garden and the other room. And so she kept to herself, for always, the moments following Aunt Harriet's call from downstairs.

"It's time to go," Maggie had said that last day to the Backwoods Girls, and she had knelt on the window seat for a final look at the garden. There was no motion at all outside; the birch leaves hung like green icicles from their branches, and, far to the left, *the broken swing hung unmoving from its single rope.*

"Maggie!" Aunt Lillian called this time.

"Okay," Maggie replied, not raising her voice.

"MAGGIE!"

"Okay!" *she shouted. "I'm coming!"*

Once more: "MAGGIE!" *and suddenly she stood frozen at the window. Who was that who called? The voice had been loud and clear, but it wasn't that of Aunt Lillian or Aunt Harriet, and it came not from the front hall but from the walls of her room. "MAGGIE!* WHATEVER IS KEEPING YOU? THE TEA IS GETTING COLD!"

*And the next moment she was out of the room and flying across the hall. It's them! It's them! and on the way she heard, in some other voice, "*SHE NEVER WAS ONE FOR GETTING PLACES ON TIME."

"I'm here," she cried breathlessly from the bottom of the attic stair. "I'm here!" from the top now, and in an instant she was rounding the wardrobe and in the doll room. "I'm here!"

Timothy John was sitting in the armchair, with the newspaper spread out on his knee. Miss Christabel was standing at the tea table, and Juniper, out of his basket, was lying at Timothy John's foot.

"Well, there you are, Maggie," Miss Christabel said, before Maggie had a chance to speak another word. "What kept you so long? We had so much to get ready, but someone very nicely took down the streamers from yesterday's party."

[313]

Yesterday's *party! Didn't they know the party had taken place weeks before?*

"*And swept up the crumbs, too,*" *Timothy John remarked, without looking up from the newspaper.*

"*Oh, Miss Christabel,*" *Maggie finally gasped.* "*Timothy John. Juniper. You're back!*"

"*What nonsense are you talking?*" *Miss Christabel said.* "*Come, give me a hand with the tea.*"

"*But I can't, Miss Christabel. I can't stay. I have to go. I'm leaving for good. I'm going to another place to live. But I'm so glad you're here and you're alive, and wherever I am I'll always think of you here, having your tea and walking in the garden and reading the paper and doing all those things you always do. Oh, Miss Christabel and Timothy John and Juniper, you're* alive!"

"*Mercy!*" *Miss Christabel exclaimed.* "*Is it time for you to leave already?*"

Timothy John slipped the gold watch out of his pocket. "*It is exactly time,*" *he said.* "*Eight thirty-five. Everything always seems to happen at eight thirty-five, so it isn't surprising that you should be leaving, Maggie.*"

"*Maybe I can come back and visit sometime,*" *Maggie said.* "*Maybe someday I'll come back to Adelphi Hills, and we can all have tea together, just as we always did—the three of us and Juniper.*"

"*Four,*" *Timothy John corrected her.*

Maggie looked at him.

"Four of us," he said. "We are three up here now. He's come, you know."

"Who's come? Where?"

"In the garden," Miss Christabel answered. "Our newcomer. The Other One."

"What other one?" Maggie's head spun back and forth. "Who?" and her eye swept across the room. There was an extra chair at the table, she now noticed, and, strangely, a third bed. Other things, too, seemed added, rearranged, and she let out a quick gasp as she caught sight of something else in the corner: a small round bowler, its crown looking as though it had just been brushed with the sleeve of a coat, hanging on the clothes hook; and, against the wall, a small walking stick, its silver knob shining like a smooth, a perfect moon.

"Four of us," he said. "We are three up here now. He's come, you know."

"Who's come? Where?"

"In the garden," Miss Christabel answered. "Our newcomer. The Other One."

"What other one?" Maggie's head spun back and forth. "Who?" and her eye swept across the room. There was an extra chair at the table, she now noticed, and, strangely, a third bed. Other things, too, seemed added, rearranged, and she let out a quick gasp as she caught sight of something else in the corner: a small round bowler, its crown looking as though it had just been brushed with the sleeve of a coat, hanging on the clothes hook; and, against the wall, a small walking stick, its silver knob shining like a smooth, a perfect moon.